ALSO BY GLENN BECK

An Inconvenient Book:
Real Solutions to the World's Biggest Problems

The Real America: Messages from the Heart and Heartland

The

Christmas

Sweater

Glenn Beck

with Kevin Balfe and Jason Wright

THRESHOLD
EDITIONS

NEW YORK   LONDON   TORONTO   SYDNEY

THRESHOLD EDITIONS
A Division of Simon & Schuster, Inc.
1230 Avenue of the Americas
New York, NY 10020

First Threshold Editions hardcover edition November 2008

THRESHOLD EDITIONS and colophon are trademarks
of Simon & Schuster, Inc.

For information about special discounts for bulk purchases,
please contact Simon & Schuster Special Sales at
1-800-456-6798 or business@simonandschuster.com.

Designed by Ruth Lee-Mui

Manufactured in the United States of America

10   9   8   7   6   5   4   3

ISBN-13: 978-1-4165-9485-7
ISBN-10:   1-4165-9485-X

For my children,

Mary, Hannah, Raphe,
and Cheyenne.

Always remember where we came from,
how we got here, and
Who led us into the warmth of the sunshine.

The Way It Ends . . .

he Christmas sweater sat on the top shelf of my closet for many years.

The sweater hadn't fit me for decades, and if I hadn't moved a lot in my earlier years, it would've never been touched. Still, I never considered giving it away. With each move I would gently fold it into a moving box and transport it to my next home, carefully placing it on another shelf, never to be worn.

No matter how much time passed, the mere sight of the sweater always invoked a powerful reaction in me. Captured in its yarn were fragments of my childhood innocence—my greatest regrets, fears, hopes, disappointments—and, in time, my greatest joy.

I began writing this story with the intention of sharing it with just my family. But something happened along the way: The story took over and wrote itself. There are things I spent years trying, and eventually succeeding, to forget that just spilled out of me—events I never intended to share with anyone. It's almost as if my sweater wanted its story told. Perhaps it had sat silent on a shelf long enough.

It has taken me more than thirty years to feel comfortable enough to share this story. I suppose it will take the rest of my life to fully understand the complete meaning and power behind it. And while some of the names and events have been changed, what follows is, at its core, the story of the most important Christmas of my life.

In the spirit of this blessed season, I share this story as my gift to you. May it bring you and your loved ones the same joy it's brought to me.

Eddie's Prayer

Lord, I know it's been a while since I talked to you last and I'm sorry.

With all that's happened it's been hard to know what to say.

Mom keeps telling me you're there watching over us, even during the bad times. I guess I believe her, but sometimes it's hard to understand why you've let all of this stuff happen to us.

I know that Mom is working hard and money is tight, but please, God, if I could just get a bike for Christmas then everything will be better. I'll do whatever you want to prove that I'm worthy. I'll go to church. I'll study hard. I'll be a good son to Mom.

I'll earn it, I promise.

One

he wipers cut semicircles through the snow on the windshield. *It's good snow,* I thought as I slid forward and rested my chin on the vinyl of the front seat.

"Sit back, honey," my mother, Mary, gently commanded. She was thirty-nine years old, but her tired eyes and the streaks of gray infiltrating her otherwise coal black hair made most people think she was much older. If your age was determined by what you'd been through in life, they would have been right.

"But Mom, I can't see the snow when I sit back."

"Okay. But just until we stop for gas."

I scooted up farther and rested my worn Keds on the hump that ran through the middle of our old Pinto station wagon. I was skinny and tall for my age, which made my knees curl up toward my chest. Mom said I was safer in the backseat, but deep down I knew that it wasn't really about safety, it was about the radio. I was constantly playing with it, changing the dial from her boring Perry Como station to something that played real music.

As we continued toward the gas station, I could see the edge of downtown Mount Vernon through the snow. A thousand points of red and green Christmas lights lined the edges of Main Street. Hot summer days in Washington State were rare, but when they happened, the light poles covered in Christmas lights seemed out of place. They hung there in a kind of backward hibernation until a city worker would plug them in and replace the bulbs that didn't wake up. But now, in December, the lights were working their magic, filling us kids with excitement for the season.

That year I was more anxious than excited. I wanted

it to be the year that Christmas finally returned to normal. For years, Christmas mornings in our home had been filled with gifts and laughter and smiling faces. But my father had died three years earlier—and it seemed to me that Christmas had died with him.

Before my father's death I didn't think much about our financial situation. We weren't wealthy, we weren't poor—we just were. We'd had a nice house in a good neighborhood, a hot dinner every night and, one summer, when I was five years old, we even went to Disneyland. I remember getting dressed up for the airplane ride. The only other vacation I remember happened a few years later when my parents took me to Birch Bay—which sounds exotic but was really just a rocky beach about an hour away from our home.

Back then we never wanted for anything, except maybe more time together.

My father bought City Bakery when I was young—it had been in town since the 1800s. He put in long hours at work, leaving almost every morning before the sun (or his son) rose. My mother would get me off to school, clean up around the house a little, start some laundry, and then join him at the bakery for the rest of the day.

After school I would walk to the bakery to help my parents out. On some days the walk took less than half an hour, but it usually took me a lot longer. At least a few days each week I would stop at the edge of downtown in the middle of the bridge that crossed the I-5 freeway and watch the cars and trucks whiz by. A lot of kids would stand there and spit onto the roadway below, hoping to hit a car, but I wasn't that kind of kid. I just imagined myself spitting.

I complained a lot about having to be at the bakery so much, especially when my dad made me wash the pots and pans, but secretly I loved to watch him work. Others might have called him a baker, but I thought of him as a master craftsman or a sculptor. Instead of a chisel he used dough, and instead of clay he used frosting—but the result was always a masterpiece.

Dad and my uncle Bob both apprenticed in their father's bakery from the time they were my age. Donning aprons, they washed a seemingly never-ending line of pots and pans, and they would learn recipes after school. In my dad's case, it wasn't long before the apprentice was more skilled than the master.

Dad just had a knack for baking. He was the only one in the family who could bring his recipes to life. It wasn't long before City Bakery's breads and desserts were known as the best in town. Dad loved his creations almost as much as he loved his family.

Saturdays were special because it was the day my father spent most of his time icing and decorating cakes. Not coincidentally, it was also the day I liked to work with him the most. Well, *work* might be a bit of an exaggeration, as I didn't do much baking myself. Taking bread out of the proof box after it had risen was about as far as he'd let me go—but I watched him closely, and I took advantage of my role as "official frosting taster" as often as possible.

Although Dad continually tried to teach me his recipes, I never quite got them down. Mom blamed it on my having the attention span of a gnat, but I knew it was really because I liked eating better than I liked baking. I was never interested in being a baker; it was too much work and you had to get up way too early. But Dad never gave up hope that one day I might change my mind.

His first mission was to teach me how to make cookies, but not long after putting me in charge of the cookie dough and mixer he realized he'd made a mistake. A big mistake. If he'd left me alone with that raw dough for just a few more minutes, he wouldn't have had enough left to bake. After that, Dad smartly switched his tactic from hands-on lessons to pop quizzes. He'd show me how to make a few batches of German chocolate cake, then he'd test me on the recipe and toss flour in my face when I invariably mentioned some ingredient that had no business being in a cake. Like meat.

One day, right in the middle of an apple-strudel quiz, Dad's cashier (my mother) came into the back to ask if he'd mind helping a customer. This wasn't entirely unusual—Dad would come up front once in a while, mainly in the afternoons while the ovens were cooling and my mom made the daily trip to the bank. I think it was secretly one of his favorite times of the day; he was a real people person, and he loved to watch the faces of his customers as they sampled his latest creation.

That day, I watched as Dad greeted Mrs. Olsen, a woman who seemed to me like the oldest person in town. She was a regular customer. When my mom waited on her, I noticed that she'd always spend a little extra time just listening to Mrs. Olsen's stories. I guess she thought Mrs. Olsen was lonely. Dad treated her with the same kind of respect. He smiled warmly as he spoke to her, and I noticed the faintest hint of a smile begin to form on her face as well. Dad had that effect on a lot of people.

7

Mrs. Olsen had come in for a single loaf of bread, but Dad spent five minutes trying to talk her into everything from his napoleons to his German chocolate cake. She kept refusing, but my dad insisted, saying it was all on him. She finally relented, and her smile stretched from ear to ear. She told him that he was too kind. I remember the word "kind" because I thought it was simple, and yet so true. My dad was kind.

After her bread had been bagged and her free treats boxed, Mrs. Olsen reached into her purse and pulled out a kind of money I'd never seen before. As far as I could tell it wasn't cash. It looked more like coupons—except we didn't offer any coupons. As she turned to leave the store, my heart began to race. Had Dad just been scammed right in front of me? The bakery paid our bills (and, more importantly, it paid for my presents). I crept up next to my father at the cash register and, not thinking she could hear me, whispered, "Dad, that's not money."

Mrs. Olsen stopped dead in her tracks and looked at my father. He, in turn, glared at me. "Eddie, into the back, please. Right now." His voice had a definite edge to it. He then gave Mrs. Olsen a sympathetic nod and another warm smile, and she turned and continued out the door. I knew I was in trouble.

As I walked through the opening into the back, my face felt hotter than the oven I was now standing in front of. "Eddie, I know you didn't mean it, but do you know how embarrassing that was for Mrs. Olsen?"

"No," I replied. I honestly didn't.

"Eddie, Mrs. Olsen is a very good customer of ours. Her husband passed away about a year ago and she's had a hard time making ends meet. You're right, what she gave me isn't money, but it's just like it for people who need it. They're called food stamps, and our government is helping her buy groceries until she can get back on her feet. We don't talk about them in front of her because she doesn't like the fact that she has to ask others for help."

Dad explained that while our family would never accept help from anyone, especially the government, there were good people who needed it. I immediately felt sorry for Mrs. Olsen—sorry for anyone who needed to rely on others for that kind of help. And I was glad that we would never be in that position.

A few months later I got a chance to prove to my father that I'd learned my lesson.

Mom had once again run to the bank, and I was in the front of the store putting fresh macaroons into the display case while Dad waited on customers. I watched as, once again, he accepted the funny-looking coupons as payment—this time from a guy buying bread, a pie, and a dozen cookies. But now, instead of warm smiles, friendly

9

conversation, and yummy dessert suggestions, my father was completely silent.

After the customer left it was my turn to do the questioning. I followed him into the back. "What's wrong, Dad?" I asked.

"I know that man, Eddie. He can work, but he chooses not to. Anyone who can earn money has no business taking it from others."

I eventually came to understand that my father, who'd grown up poor and struggled for everything we owned, had continually rejected offers of help from others. He had worked hard to build a business and provide for his family. He believed others should do the same. "The government," he told me one night, "is there to act as a safety net, not a candy machine."

I don't know if my mother had grown up with the same attitude or if she'd just learned it from all those years with my dad—but she felt the exact same way. With him now gone we were really struggling, but she refused to consider asking anyone for help. "We'll get through this,

Eddie," she told me more than once. "Things are just a little tight right now, but there are so many others who need it more than we do."

As usual, Mom was being an optimist. "A little tight" didn't begin to describe how frugal we had become. When we went out to dinner, which was only on very special occasions, she would always give me the same warning before the waitress appeared: "Remember, Eddie, don't order any milk, we have plenty of it at home. No need to be wasteful."

I knew better. It wasn't about waste, it was about money. That was all it was ever about. Mom worked seemingly endless hours at a seemingly endless number of jobs, our house was crumbling faster than Dad's famous apple turnovers, and I hadn't gotten a brag-worthy Christmas present since the Star Wars Millennium Falcon I'd gotten two years earlier.

But this year would be different. I had been on my best behavior for months now. I'd taken out the garbage before Mom had asked, used my finely honed dishwashing skills at home, and had generally made sure that she wouldn't have any excuse to not get me the bike I deserved.

Still, I wasn't leaving anything to chance. Every time a relative or neighbor asked what I wanted for Christmas, I made sure my mother was close enough to hear my finely tuned response: A red Huffy bike with a black banana seat.

12

The Ford's loud motor snapped me out of yesterday's memories. We were on Main Street, and the once distant lights now glowed brightly through our foggy windows. I tried to look out the back windshield to see where we were, but I could only see my mop of dirty-blond hair reflecting back.

Mom drove cautiously, although downtown seemed to be virtually deserted. A light turned red at the intersection ahead, and she slowly eased the car to a stop.

"Eddie, look!" She was pointing out the passenger-side window.

I rubbed my hand back and forth on the glass to clear the condensation. We had come to a stop right outside Richmond's Sporting Goods' big storefront window, the very place I had first seen the Huffy I'd been dreaming about all year.

My eyes expertly searched the window, darting from baseball bats to gloves to sleds to . . . there it was. The Huffy. *My* Huffy. Its bright red frame, shiny chrome handlebars, and black banana seat sparkled brilliantly through the snow and fog.

"Wow." It was the only word I could come up with.

Mom wasn't looking at the bike anymore, she was looking at me in the rearview mirror. I couldn't see her mouth, but I knew that she was smiling. I smiled back. Perry Como provided the sound track.

"You want to pump the gas?" she asked a few minutes later as she pulled up to the self-service island. We stopped for gas a lot because our Pinto was always thirsty and Mom usually only had enough money to fill the tank partway.

"Sure," I said, leaping over the seat and following her

out the door. "Can I get some Red Vines when I go in to pay?"

"I'm sorry, Eddie," my mother said gently. "I have the money for Red Vines but not enough for the dentist." She smiled. "Now, scoot." I knew she didn't have money for the dentist, but her excuse didn't fool me. I knew she didn't have money for Red Vines either.

I gave her the best look of disappointment I could muster. Still, deep down, I had hope. No money for Red Vines could mean that she was saving it all for something else.

14

My bike.

Two

t was Christmas Eve, and, as usual, Mom was at work. She was a cook at the local high school, but she always picked up an extra job or two at the mall around the holidays.

I was home from school by myself, which always made Mom anxious. She hated leaving me alone. Not because I couldn't take care of myself, but because she knew that I was way too much like my mischievous grandfather—who happened to be the inventor of the very pre-Christmas tradition that I was about to embark on: Operation Sneak Preview.

One Christmas Eve, a few years ago, Grandpa and I found ourselves alone. My father was still at the bakery finishing up the croissants and cakes that would soon elicit "oohs" and "ahhs" at dinner tables all across town. My mom and grandma had gone to church. Normally my grandpa and I would've been dragged along, but Christmas was on a Monday that year, and somehow he had persuaded them that tomorrow's Christmas service should count for both days. I had a lot to learn from him.

"You want to play cards, Eddie?" Grandpa asked as soon as the front door clicked shut.

18

Oh boy, here we go again, I thought.

Grandpa loved playing cards. No, I take that back, he loved *winning* at cards. And he always won. In fact, he won so often that it had become somewhat of an unwritten family rule that you never, ever, at any cost, agreed to play cards with him. It was like feeding a wild animal: It might seem like a good idea at first, but you always regretted it later.

I used to believe that Grandpa won at cards because he was really good, but that year I was old enough to know better. He won because he cheated. Perhaps "cheated" isn't the right word; Grandpa had a system. Much like counting cards at a blackjack table, his methods weren't necessarily illegal, but he didn't advertise them either.

Whenever we played, he concentrated more on figuring out the holes in his system than on actually beating me—though that never posed much of a problem either. I'd play a card and he'd pick it up and put it back in my hand and say, "Nope. You don't want to play that card." At first I thought he was just being helpful, but later I realized that it wasn't about the kill for him. It was about the thrill of the chase. For Grandpa, playing cards with me was like going on a big-game hunt at the zoo—there was no real sport involved. I never really felt like I was playing cards with Grandpa so much as I was his test subject.

I always figured that he used the practice rounds with me to refine his system so that he could win his weekly card game with friends, but I never asked and he never told me.

"You're sure you don't want to play?" he repeated.

"Sorry, Grandpa. Maybe later."

19

"Suit yourself. But I'm feeling pretty vulnerable today. I think you might have a real shot at beating me." Grandpa was a *really* good liar. "But if you're sure you don't want to play cards . . ." His voice lowered as he got that "I'm more of a kid than you are" glint in his eyes. "Maybe I can think of something else for us to do."

"What?" I asked, which really meant "I'm in!" Grandpa had a knack for getting us into various levels of trouble, and I loved every second of it. His "ideas" were almost always code word for an elaborate plot he'd spent weeks dreaming up. As evidenced by his secret card-counting system, Grandpa was a big fan of finding the gray area between the letter of the law and the spirit of it.

"Follow me," he said, the playful edge in his voice now completely gone. Grandpa took his schemes very seriously. Whenever he and I embarked on a mission, no matter how absurd it was, we tried as hard as possible to get away with it. On the rare occasions when we did get caught, he would skillfully employ an extraordinarily complex, time-tested strategy: Deny, deny, deny. Surprisingly, it worked most of the time because adults simply didn't want to believe a grown man would actually do the things he did.

A great example occurred two summers earlier, when a troublemaking teenager stayed with his aunt, who lived across the street from my grandparents. The demon kid would stay up late screaming and hollering, vandalizing mailboxes, and generally trying to make life miserable for everyone in the usually quiet neighborhood.

His favorite activity took place after dark, when he would set up a wall of rocks across the country road that wound its way through the neighborhood. Placed right at the crest of a small hill, the wall was invisible to cars coming from either direction. It wasn't high—just a few inches in most places—but that was enough to make the unlucky cars that hit it blow out a tire, lose a muffler, or worse.

The first few times it happened, the neighbors called the police. But that did little good, because no one actually caught the kid with the rocks. After a while most people just kept quiet and counted down the days until the unwelcome visitor would leave. But not Grandpa.

A few days after the first rock wall incident, he began plotting. He observed that every night, after the mayhem was over, the kid would leave his football on his aunt's front porch. The next morning, while Grandpa was eating breakfast, he would watch as the kid would run outside barefoot and kick his ball into the yard as hard as he could. That routine gave my grandpa a simple, yet completely diabolical, idea.

One night, while the rest of the neighborhood slept, Grandpa took the football from the porch and brought it into his workshop. He carefully slit it open and filled it with the same rocks and stones the kid had used to make his walls. Then he sealed it back up and returned it to the porch.

I don't know exactly what happened after that, but I do know that the kid had a cast on his foot the next afternoon and the neighborhood never heard another peep out of him.

No one ever knew my grandpa was responsible.

While I never knew when he'd pulled another prank, I always figured that something had happened when he provided me with an alibi for no apparent reason. During a walk to the barn or a trip into town he'd turn to me and say something cryptic like, "By the way, Eddie, if anyone asks, you and I were at the feed store last night around six." I'd smile and never have to ask why.

The only two people who would ever call him on his schemes were my mother and my grandma. They knew that Grandpa was the *only* one who would ever go through all the trouble of flawlessly filling a football with rocks just to teach someone a lesson. But he didn't cave easily. When it became clear that his denials would not stand up, he would say, "Eddie might have been slightly involved in something like that."

While it might sound like he was simply shifting the blame to me, that's only part of the story. The real reason Grandpa loved to use that defense is that his name was Edward too. When he said "Eddie did it," people would naturally assume that he meant me, and he could still feel good for not *technically* lying. Fortunately anyone who really knew my grandpa wasn't fooled, so I never got in trouble.

23

Now, back in the farmhouse, in the early stages of carrying out yet another undercover mission, Grandpa walked with a purpose. I did the best I could to keep up, but my short legs had to take two steps for every one of his long, graceful strides. We didn't stop until we were standing in front of the guest bedroom closet. Without a word, Grandpa pulled open the closet door and reached one of his long arms into the back corner, retrieving a wrapped present. I was speechless.

"First thing a Christmas aficionado needs to learn," he said firmly, "is that the good presents never go under the tree until Christmas morning."

My eyes grew wide as his arm dashed back behind the clothes hamper and another present, this one slightly larger than the first, materialized. "Ooh, Grandma's getting sly," he snickered, clearly proud of himself. Four gifts later he was done fishing. "Okay, Eddie, now hold this one up to your ear. What do you think it is?"

I took the box, careful not to rip the wrapping paper or crush the bow. The tag on the front said, "To Grandpa,

From Grandma." I held it up to my ear, unsure of exactly what I was supposed to be listening for. "Hmm . . ." I pretended to be weighing various options in my head, though the truth was I didn't even have a guess. "I don't know. I don't really hear much."

"Let me have a shot," he said, barely able to control his excitement.

I handed the box to him and he put it against the side of his head. He closed his eyes, shook it lightly, paused, then announced his verdict: "It's a winter coat. Brown."

"Really?" I was shocked. "How do you know?"

"I can hear it. Now hand me that one."

I picked up a rectangular box, put it in his oversized hands, and watched as he repeated the same process: Listen, shake, pause, verdict. "This is a curling iron. One of the fancy ones that automatically turns itself off."

I was stunned. Not about the curling iron, but at hearing how sure Grandpa was about it. There wasn't an ounce of doubt in his voice.

He asked me for the other two presents and repeated

25

the now familiar routine. I put the curling iron and coat box to my ear as he worked, trying to hear something, *anything*, but they were both silent.

Grandpa sat on the floor next to a present he'd decided was a new teapot for my mom. "Come here, Eddie, and sit next to me for a second. I want to teach you something. There is an art to Christmas." He smiled, magic dancing in his eyes. "Some might say what I am about to show you is a dark art, but I prefer to think of it more as green and red."

26

I slid over next to him.

"I believe it's time that you finally understand the truth about the magic of Christmas."

"Grandpa, I already know. I'm not a little kid anymore."

"That's not what I'm talking about. The magic itself is real, but sometimes it needs to be 'helped' along a bit. And that's what I am . . . 'a helper.' It's like your dad's bread. The yeast and flour may rise on their own, but nothing happens unless your dad puts it in the oven. That's me. I'm like a Christmas-present oven." This was my grandfather at his very best.

Without waiting to see if I understood his cryptic analogy, he picked up the square present, turned it over, and exhaled gently at the seam where a single piece of tape held the paper flap shut. The tape's surface fogged up from the humidity of his breath. He then worked gently at the corner of the tape with his fingernail until he was satisfied that he could peel it away without ripping the paper. The flap opened flawlessly.

My eyes must've been as big as bike wheels as I watched what happened next: Grandpa put the gift on the carpet, reached his hand in through the open flap and gently slid the box out. Then he handed it to me. "Open it," he said. "But be careful."

I pulled the top open, removed the red tissue paper, and found the present—a ceramic, oriental teapot with four small cups. Just what my mother wanted and just what my grandpa had predicted, though it was now obvious that it hadn't been a prediction so much as a fact.

27

We moved on to the other gifts. Some had multiple pieces of tape, which required patience; my grandpa reminded me that that was a virtue. Others were wrapped so tightly that you had to turn them upside down to get the box out. One by one, we unwrapped and rewrapped them all. (I later learned that by the time Christmas rolled around, my grandfather had opened all of his gifts *at least* three times.) After we finished, he carefully returned each present to its original hiding place, and we went downstairs.

28

Little did I know that we weren't even close to being done.

Underneath the Christmas tree, there was a treasure trove of wrapped gifts to explore. We opened them all. It didn't matter who they were to, or who they were from. We opened them, talked about them, and sometimes even played with them. Then we sealed them all up and carefully placed them back under the tree, exactly how we'd found them.

Grandpa swore me to secrecy, but he didn't need to. I knew that Operation Sneak Preview would provide

Christmas magic for years to come, and I wasn't about to blow it. My grandfather might have been the master, but just as my father had learned how to bake, I quickly became my grandfather's very skilled apprentice.

With my mom still at work for at least another couple of hours, I had plenty of time to execute this year's "operation."

Mom and I had been in a continual, although unspoken, game of cat and mouse for the last few Christmases. She'd find a great hiding spot and I'd find her great hiding spot. She'd find a better spot and I'd find that one too. Maybe I hadn't been as skilled as I'd thought in regards to putting the presents back exactly how I'd found them, because she'd always seemed to know when her hiding places had been compromised.

This year, as I started searching the floor of her bedroom closet, I was determined not to leave the slightest trace. After all, I was twelve now and sure that I could finally pull off the "operation" as well as Grandpa.

29

As my hand felt into the back corner of the closet, I realized that I was secretly hoping I *wouldn't* find a present there. If my present could fit in a closet, then there was no way it could be a bike, and that was the *only* gift I wanted that year. What I was hoping to find was a receipt—and I knew Mom would be smart enough to hide that too.

My hands carefully searched every nook and cranny of the closet floor. And then I felt it. A box. Small. Unwrapped. "Ooh, Mom's slipping," I laughed to myself as I pulled the box out from the darkness. A thin layer of dust coated the top. How had I missed this the last few years?

I pulled the top off gently, careful not to leave fingerprints in the dust just in case this was an elaborate trap set by my mother. As I pushed the tissue paper out of the way, I realized immediately that it was not. The item inside was instantly familiar. It was my dad's favorite old Hamilton watch. A faint hint of his Old Spice cologne still resonated from the band.

Without warning, my mind flashed to an image of the last time I saw that watch. It was about four years ago, right after a morning snowstorm had delayed the start of school. It was a Monday, and the bakery was closed. Dad was home, hunched over in front of me as he secured clear plastic bread bags over my shoes. My friends had real winter boots, but my father said they were a waste of money since we had so many free bread bags around the house that could do the job just as well. That should have been a clue that we weren't exactly the Rockefellers—but it made sense to me at the time.

As he worked a rubber band over my shoes to fasten the bag tightly onto my skinny calves, his shirtsleeve pulled up, revealing the shiny Hamilton watch. I stared at the time, realizing that I was now seriously late for school and dreading the prospect of hurrying over slushy snow with slippery plastic bags on my feet. They might have kept the water out, but they weren't known for their traction.

"Dad, I've really got to go. I'm gonna be late," I'd insisted, hoping that he'd give up on the homemade waterproofing and drive me instead.

"Sorry, Eddie, I'd rather you be late than have to sit through school with cold, wet feet. I just need another second."

I'd stared at the Hamilton, watching the small second hand go round and round, each revolution marking how much faster I would have to run to make it on time.

I'd also thought about how ironic it was that my dad was a baker and though we had plenty of bread bags, we never had any bread in the house.

"Eddie," he would say to me, "if I bring all my bread home for us to eat, then what am I supposed to sell?"

It was a funny line, but I knew it was an excuse. The truth was that after a long day at work, my parents would rush to close up and simply forget to bring home the bread they had been staring at all day. My mother thought it was hilarious. She used to joke that the cobbler's son never had any shoes to wear and the butcher's son never had any steak to eat, so we were even, but I never found it that funny.

I had gotten so accustomed to not having bread at home that I once dumped an entire jar of peanut butter into a bowl and started eating it with a spoon. My mother came into the kitchen and did a double take.

"What the heck are you doing?" she asked, genuinely shocked to see the heaping spoonfuls I was shoveling into my mouth.

"What do you mean?" I answered as best I could, considering the fact that I was unable to fully open my mouth. "We have no bread."

"That's no excuse for you to eat like an animal. Now put that away."

I snuck a couple more spoonfuls after she left, then scooped the rest of it back into the jar. Fortunately Mom had only chastised me about peanut-butter eating, so other condiments were still fair game. For the next few weeks I enjoyed bowls full of Marshmallow Fluff, strawberry jam, and even whipped cream. Then I tried mayonnaise; with that, my breadless-condiment-sampling experiment officially came to a disgusting end.

Dad finally finished tying on my bread-bag boots, and I rushed through the front door into the cold. Being late for school gave me a great excuse to run, but my real intention was to get out of sight as fast as possible so I could rip the stupid bags off my feet. I once made the mistake of

33

showing up at school with them on, and it took months before my friends stopped making fun of me. "Bread Bag Ed" was my first nickname, but that quickly turned into the far more memorable "Breaddie Eddie." It was spring before everyone forgot the incident. I wasn't eager to help them remember.

The Hamilton's second hand, which had once symbolized how badly I'd wanted to flee from my father that snowy winter's day, now sat there idly, mocking me. I wished I hadn't run so quickly to school that day. Time didn't seem to matter anymore.

I carefully put the watch back into its box, replaced the tissue paper, then returned it to its original resting place. I wondered how such a powerful memory of my father could be stored in a dark and lonely closet, but it seemed fitting.

Before moving on to more inventive hiding spots, I decided to check under the obvious one: my mother's bed. It was a long shot, but I wouldn't be able to live with myself if my gift was that close and I missed it.

I got down on my stomach and squirmed under the bed skirt and into the darkness. My eyes took a few seconds to adjust, but once they did, everything looked familiar. A few shoe boxes, leaves to extend the dining room table, a sewing kit, and . . . wait, what was that? There was a box I'd never seen before. It was good sized and shiny. I marked its exact position before pulling it out into the light.

The box was wider than a shoe box and much deeper. A label on the top, written in my mom's handwriting, said simply, "Christmas Receipts." Could this really be it? Could it be this easy? My hands shook in anticipation.

I gently pulled the top off and peered inside. There was only one receipt. *Don't be disappointed*, I thought to myself. *One bike, one receipt.* I unfolded the receipt quickly, hoping to read "Richmond's" printed across the top, but there was no store name. In fact, there wasn't an item description, a price, or even a date. Instead, there was a handwritten note:

35

Hi Mister Nosey. You can stop looking. Your present has been right underneath your nose the whole time, but you'll never find it.

This couldn't be happening. Mom had not only used reverse psychology on me but she'd also beaten me with it. Grandpa would be so disappointed. *Grandpa.* A vision of him teaching me proper Scotch tape removal suddenly filled my mind. He would never have been defeated this easily. I felt a renewed energy. I might have lost this battle, but I wouldn't lose the war.

I refolded Mom's note along its original crease lines, placed it back into the box, and slid it under the bed and into its original position. If my mother didn't know I found her note, then I hadn't technically lost. With just a little luck, my dignity and my grandpa's honor could still be saved.

Three

t's funny how life changes so fast. A few years earlier, money had been the last thing on my mind. Now it was all I thought about. A few years earlier, I'd had a father. Now he was gone. A few years earlier, I'd loved going caroling with my mom every Christmas Eve. Now I couldn't think of anything worse.

It's hard being a twelve-year-old kid. It's even harder being a twelve-year-old kid whose mother seems to be on a mission from God to embarrass you. At least that's how I felt that Christmas Eve.

"Mom, please don't make me go. I'm really too old for this." I already knew arguing was a lost cause.

"Come on, Eddie, you always have fun. The ladies love to see you. Besides, how will they update your height on their door frame if you don't show up?"

Mom was smiling, but I felt like I was walking a tightrope. Too much protesting and she might make me wait past Christmas for my bike.

"Fine. But can we at least keep it short? I want to have enough energy to say all my prayers tonight." I hadn't used the "prayers excuse" in years, but I hoped she cared more about my prayers than she did about caroling.

Her smile vanished. Uh-oh. "Eddie, your sudden devotion to God is inspiring, but believe me, God will be more than happy to hear your prayers no matter how much energy you have. Now go get the Wonder Bread bags and get yourself ready to go."

This was quickly going from bad to worse. I never thought that my father's bread-bag boots could somehow be made *more* embarrassing, but after he died my mother found a way: Wonder Bread bag boots. I now not only got to wear cheap plastic bags over my shoes but I got to wear cheap plastic bags *with multicolored polka dots* over my shoes. It was a complete and total nightmare.

"I don't need those tonight," I said firmly. "We're getting right into the car."

"It's not negotiable, Eddie. It's slushy out there and I can't have you wearing wet shoes all night. You might get sick for Christmas."

Someone needed to give my mom a serious lesson on viruses. Even I knew that you couldn't catch a cold from the cold, but somehow a health lesson didn't seem like the smartest reply. I made the right decision and held my tongue.

41

"Okay, I'll put them on."

I was looking for the bags under the kitchen sink when I heard the doorbell ring. Our front door swung open and the unintelligible noise that only occurs when two grown women get together reverberated through the house. Aunt Cathryn had arrived.

I was nine before I understood that "Aunt" Cathryn wasn't really my aunt—she was actually just our next-door neighbor. Her kids were grown and had left home, so she had adopted us as her family. But family or not, she was without a doubt the nicest person I knew, and my mother always seemed happy when she was with her.

I reluctantly carried my Wonder Bread bags into the family room and sat on the couch, awaiting the inevitable sequence of events that was about to transpire.

"Edddddddie, how are you?" Aunt Cathryn violently pinched my cheeks. I hated that. "Merry Christmas!" No one had ever accused her of being shy.

42

"I'm great, Aunt Cathryn, how are you?"

"I'm always great, Eddie, but thanks for asking. I just can't believe it's time for Christmas caroling again. I feel like we just did it!"

That's the understatement of the century, I thought to myself. For the second time that evening I held my tongue.

"Oh, and look at your tree. It's beautiful!"

Aunt Cathryn had more energy than anyone else I'd ever met. If you measured the importance of a sentence by how enthusiastically it was said, Aunt Cathryn might as well have been president. But her voice suddenly became uncharacteristically soft. "But where's the star?"

While there were decorations everywhere else on the tree, the top was bare. The star that usually resided there was missing because no one was tall enough to put it in place—a constant reminder that something, or rather *someone*, was also missing.

"I'll take care of it," I offered, not wanting to get into a discussion about my dad on Christmas Eve. I removed our stepladder from the hall closet and unfolded it next to the tree. Then I went back to the closet and retrieved a simple white star from its box. I returned to the ladder, climbed to the top step, steadied myself, and clipped the star into place. Aunt Cathryn smiled.

"Well, Eddie," my mother said, "I guess that officially makes you the man of the house."

It was obvious that she regretted the words before they'd even escaped her mouth. Aunt Cathryn and I both stared at the floor in awkward silence, but we were think-ing the same thing: There was nothing we wanted less.

After I put on my Wonder Bread bags and looked sufficiently ridiculous, the three of us piled into our car for the drive to the nursing home. We had caroled there every Christmas Eve for the last five or six years.

The one saving grace was that we caroled inside, out of view. It would have been bad enough to be seen by my friends singing Christmas carols with my mother, but throw in Wonder Bread bags and Aunt Cathryn, and "Breaddie Eddie" would have seemed like a dream compared to the torment that would've come my way.

My mother drove mind-numbingly slowly as Aunt Cathryn wore out the tuner knob on the car radio. After five straight minutes of static intermingled with ten-second song clips, I finally had enough.

"Any chance we could stick to one station?" I asked. When it came to keeping my mouth shut, the third time wasn't the charm.

"Sure. Sorry, Eddie," Aunt Cathryn replied. "I was just

looking for a Christmas song so that we could all practice our harmony."

I let out an involuntary laugh. "Harmony? If you think we have any harmony, then you must be as deaf as our audience."

Strike two.

I looked up and locked eyes with my mother, who was now glaring at me in the rearview mirror. She could give a full lecture by just using her eyes, that's how intense they were. And right now they were telling me to sit back and keep quiet.

45

"MOM!" Traffic up ahead was at a dead stop. She turned her attention back to the road and slammed on the brakes. We screeched to a stop just inches from the rear bumper of the car in front of us. Mom's eyes once again met mine in the mirror, but this time there was no anger, only concern.

"Eddie, are you okay?"

"I'm fine, Mom." I felt responsible. My stupid joke had distracted her.

"It looks like there's an accident up ahead. I'm really glad we're not part of it."

We were at a near standstill, just barely creeping along. A cacophony of car horns blared intermittently, drowning out the Christmas song that was playing on the radio.

About twenty minutes later we finally saw police flares and flashing lights pass. The cars had been cleared from the scene, but broken glass still littered the road. I looked into the mirror and saw my mother's head bow as she quietly whispered a prayer.

Once we got past the crash site, traffic flowed freely, but by then we were in danger of missing the caroling.

"What do you think, Eddie, should we just head home?" Mom asked.

I liked the fact that she thought I was old enough to have a vote. My first instinct was to say, "Yeah, let's just go home." But then I realized this was an opportunity to help my mom forget about my two-strike count.

"Nah, let's keep going," I replied confidently. "Even if we miss caroling, we can still say hello to everyone."

Impressed, my mother glanced back at me. Her eyes once again said it all: I'd answered correctly.

A few minutes later we pulled into the parking lot at the nursing home. Though I knew no one would see me during the forty-second walk to the front door, I still felt uneasy.

The nursing home was uncomfortably warm, and there was a rather "distinctive" smell. As we walked down the hallway to the lounge, I could hear the other carolers singing. At first it was just muted tones, but as we got closer I began to make out the words to "God Be with You Till We Meet Again."

47

It was about as far from a Christmas song as you could get, but my dad had always insisted that it be the last song we sang each year. He said that mentions of Santa Claus and snow were great, but leaving people with the spirit of Christmas was what really mattered—and that song never failed to do it. I tried to protest the first year, but when I looked up and saw the tears in the eyes of our audience as we sang, I knew Dad was right.

God be with you 'til we meet again;
By His counsels guide, uphold you;
With His sheep securely fold you;
God be with you 'til we meet again.

We stopped singing that song after Dad died—
everyone knew it would be too hard for Mom and me
to hear it. But our late arrival this year had given the
others a window of opportunity to sing it without us there.
Now, as the familiar words took on a new and unfamiliar
meaning, a series of uninvited memories rushed into my
mind.

I was six. Dad lifted me up so I could put the star on
top of our Christmas tree.

I was seven. Dad set up my new train set and played
with me all day—and he never complained when I asked
him to say "choo choo."

I was eight. Dad bought me my first Nerf football. We
played in our snow-covered backyard until he got too tired
to run. He was getting tired a lot lately.

I was nine. We opened presents in Dad's hospital

room. Mom said the chemo made him too weak to come home. He squeezed my hand and told me that we would play catch again soon. I didn't let him see me cry.

Months flashed by in an instant and I was at my father's funeral. He looked peaceful and healthier than he had been in over a year. It didn't seem fair. The choir sang his favorite song.

> *God be with you 'til we meet again;*
> *'Neath His wings protecting hide you;*
> *Daily manna still provide you;*
> *God be with you 'til we meet again.*

49

"Eddie? Are you coming in?"
I was standing in the hallway by myself.
"Everyone wants to see you."
The carolers were still singing inside.

The lounge looked and smelled exactly like it did every year. Snowflakes cut out of construction paper hung on the walls, and an overly decorated and undersized Christmas tree inhabited the far left corner. On a folding card table, a full bowl of red punch sat untouched.

"Eddie!"

I'd barely gotten through the doorway. "Hi, Mrs. Benson."

Mrs. Benson was charging toward me, the wheels on her walker spinning over the linoleum, with several other familiar faces not far behind. I knew that more cheek pinching was inevitable. I wondered at what age a boy outgrew this humiliation.

A few minutes later the hugs, handshakes, and "Look how big Eddie has gotten!" comments had finally subsided. My cheeks were sore, but it felt good to be around so many people who wanted to be around me.

"So, Eddie, what do you want for Christmas this year?" Mrs. Benson seemed to pride herself on being the first to ask me that question every year. Usually I told her I wasn't sure, but with Mom sitting just a few feet away, I took it as my final opportunity to make sure my message had been heard loud and clear.

"A red Huffy bike with a black banana seat," I answered, a little louder than necessary.

"What a nice idea," Mrs. Benson replied, clearly surprised that after so many years I finally had a specific answer. "It's about time you got a bike. You deserve one after all you've been through."

She has no idea, I thought to myself. *Not only do I deserve a bike, I've earned it.*

After about two hours of warm smiles and off-key singing, we pulled out of the nursing home's parking lot and drove home. I could lie and say that the night had seemed to last an eternity, but the truth is that it had actually gone by too fast. I had forgotten how much I liked being with the people there. They helped me feel the Christmas spirit and forget how much I missed my father, not to mention our struggle with money and my bread-bag boots. It's funny how it felt best to be a kid around a group of really old people.

My mother had a sixth sense about "I told you so" stuff, and she wasted no time confirming her suspicions. "Not as bad as you thought, right, honey?"

51

"I guess not." I wasn't about to cave.

"Life is what you make of it. There's always fun and laughs right under your nose if you're willing to open your eyes to see it."

Mom and I locked eyes again. I had a hard time reading her this time. I didn't know if she was simply trying to reinforce her life lesson or if she was trying to bait me into admitting that I'd seen her note under the bed. I stayed silent and looked away.

"Most times we're so focused on what we think we want that we can't appreciate how happy we already are," she continued. "It's only when we forget about our problems and help others forget theirs that we realize how good we really have it."

I knew she was right, but I was far more interested in getting ready for bed than I was in having a deep conversation. It was Christmas Eve, and I was just hours away from getting the bike that would change my life.

I slipped upstairs, brushed my teeth as quickly as possible, and put on my homemade Christmas pajamas. They were periwrinkle. Even though I wouldn't want anyone to see me in them, it made me a little sad to think that this would probably be the last time I would get to wear them. Every Christmas my grandmother gave me a new set, and while pajamas couldn't compete with a bike, they were the one present that I could count on loving every year. Better still, whenever I put my pajamas on, I thought of her. She was like a redwood tree—strong and quiet, and I always felt safe in the shade of her love.

"Mom," I began carefully as I slid under the covers, "I'm twelve. Do you still have to tuck me in?"

"Yes, sir, I do."

"But I'm almost a man." I suppose the words would have had more impact if I hadn't been saying them from under a Star Wars bedspread.

"I imagine the day will come when we both know it's time for a change. I don't 'tuck you in' anymore, by the way, young *man*. I just sit with you for a few minutes and say goodnight. There's a difference."

"Okay."

"Besides, I want to talk to you about the nursing home tonight. I know you heard the song."

Sleep and Christmas morning were so close. The last thing I wanted was another one of my mom's life lessons. "What song?"

She ignored my halfhearted attempt at pleading ignorance. "Your father first sang that song to me at the end of our first date. "Til we meet, 'til we meet, God be with you 'til we meet again.'" She laughed. "He had a horrible voice. The sound of it made me cringe, but I thought it was the sweetest thing ever. Of course, when I told Grandma what he'd done, she melted. 'He's a keeper,' she told me, as if singing one church hymn could somehow make a man perfect. I didn't have the heart to tell her that Dad had probably heard that song on the radio, not at church."

54

I did my best to show absolutely no emotion. I figured that if Mom was good at speaking with her eyes, then she was probably pretty good at reading them too, and I didn't want to give her any encouragement to keep talking. But it didn't work; she kept talking.

"I watched you out in the hallway as you listened to the song. I know it made you miss Dad. I miss him too. More and more every single day. But he's not really gone.

He's here right now watching over you. His arms are around you."

As usual, my mother was right. I did miss Dad. I missed him a lot. Maybe I had been too young to realize what I'd had when he was alive, or maybe he'd just worked too much, but now, in hindsight, what I had lost was perfectly clear. And it *really* hurt.

"But honey," my mother continued, "you're missing what that song is really all about. You're missing the most important part and the whole reason Dad loved to sing it so much." She began to quietly hum the words. "'When life's perils thick confound you, put His arms unfailing round you.'" She paused for a few moments. "His arms are always around you, Eddie. And they were always around Dad too. Whenever he had a tough day at work, I sang those words to him and all would be well."

By that point my attempts to remain emotionless failed. A tear escaped my left eye and rolled down my cheek. I hoped my mother wouldn't see it, but that was unlikely.

"Besides, if God wasn't here with both of us right now,

then why would we have this beautiful night sky? Look at the clouds, Eddie. They're full of snow. And when God squeezes them from heaven tonight, we're going to have the kind of white Christmas your father always loved." She smiled at me with extra love in her doe-brown eyes and added, "So, goodnight. Try to sleep, and don't get up before daylight." She winked. "Christmas morning doesn't start until it's *morning.*"

She turned out the light as she left the room, and my night-light lit up brightly, reminding me that I wasn't quite a man just yet.

I stared out the window, determined not to fall asleep until I saw the first snowflake. The lines that my mother had gently hummed were stuck in my head. *When life's perils thick confound you, put His arms unfailing round you.* She was probably right, but I still felt alone with my burdens. I was a twelve-year-old kid with no father and no money.

As I continued gazing out the window, waiting for the storm to begin, I had no idea that soon I would need His arms more than I ever thought possible.

The storm of my life was already forming.

Four

he smell of Mom's pancakes was so wonder-
fully strong that it actually woke me up.

I jumped out of bed and rushed to the window. There's something magical about falling asleep with the ground bare and dry and waking up to it covered in a fluffy white blanket of snow.

But the magic would have to wait for some other day, because the front yard was still covered with the same coarse, gray snow that had fallen days earlier. I looked up toward the sky. The stubborn clouds still looked like they harbored snow, but so far they'd been unwilling to part with it.

The worst part was that I knew Mom wouldn't sympathize with my disappointment. She was always one of those people who thought that snow was more of a hassle than anything else. She liked the *idea* of snow, but she hated almost everything else about it. Shoveling it was a pain, the car's windshield took forever to defrost, and driving in even the smallest amount of snow was virtually out of the question. I used to tell her that she was a snow-Grinch until I became old enough to shovel and finally understood what she meant.

60

But if Mom was a Grinch, then Dad was the mayor of Whoville. No amount of snow was ever enough. We would stay up late together waiting for a promised snowstorm to start, drinking hot chocolate and listening to the radio to see if they'd cancel school early.

On days like that Christmas morning, when the weathermen had obviously been so wrong, I would get frustrated and ask Dad how, with all this technology, they couldn't even figure out if it would snow or not. It was a rhetorical question, but one time he gave me an answer that I'll never forget. "Eddie," he said, "if I baked bread as well as those morons predict the weather, our bakery would be bankrupt and we'd never have a loaf of bread in the house."

I tried hard not to laugh. It took Dad a moment before he realized what he'd just said. He paused for a second, saw the smile on my face, then said, "Well, if that were the case, then we still wouldn't have any bread, but you also wouldn't have any nice boots to wear." It was one of the few times I ever laughed at my bakery boots.

On the rare occasions when the weathermen actually got it right, Dad would wake me up early in the morning, right after he'd come back from frying the doughnuts at the bakery. All he would have to say was, "Eddie, look out the window!" and I would jump out of bed and lean against the windowsill. Dad would put his hand on top of my head and the two of us would just stand there in silence watching the snow fall.

There was one storm that I'll never forget. It began early in the afternoon, and by evening it was snowing so hard that school had already been canceled for the next day. Mom the Grinch couldn't believe it. *How can they can-*

61

cel school so early? *The snow could stop at any second and then they'll took foolish!* Dad and I tried our best to ignore her. We were like a mini snow-support group, and we didn't want her to spoil our party.

After dark we suited up and decided to take a completely unnecessary trip to the B and H corner store, about three blocks away. We went out the side door into the garage, where Dad's big maroon 1972 Impala station wagon with fake wood paneling sat waiting. Dad had bought the car "almost new" in 1974 and had been so proud when he'd first brought it home.

Our Impala was the perfect car for a kid, because it was so "modern" and full of "technology." The tailgate didn't swing out like everyone else's station wagon because this one was curved and electric. With just the push of a button the window magically disappeared up into the roof and the tailgate slid into the floor. It even had a third row of seats that faced backward. In retrospect, the tanklike Impala probably hadn't been the best car to buy at the height of the oil crisis, but maybe that's why we'd been able to afford it.

"We're not taking the car," Dad exclaimed as he saw me walking toward it. Then he bent down, grabbed the metal garage door handle, and pulled it up. "We're gonna walk."

As the door creaked open, it was like we were staring out at a dream world. The snow was still falling, but it was so light, so fluffy, that it hit the ground with just a whisper. The air was crisp and fresh with just the slightest hint of smoke from the wood fires keeping our neighbors warm.

The streetlights gave everything a surreal, peaceful glow. The snow seemed to be falling much harder in the glow of the bulbs than anywhere else, but I knew it was just an illusion.

63

Dad took my hand, and we walked down our short driveway toward the street. I instinctively tried to make the turn to where the sidewalk would be, but Dad pulled me straight ahead into the street. I didn't say a word.

We walked down the middle of the road, hand in hand, without ever seeing a car. Each time we'd pass under a streetlight I'd look up and see the yellowish glow light up the thin layer of snow on Dad's heavy wool jacket. We both looked at each other and smiled—there was no Grinch around to spoil our fun.

It was all so perfect. Actually, it was all *too* perfect—I should've known that it wouldn't last.

I felt so let down by the lack of snow that Christmas morning that I hadn't even noticed how cold the floor was. I put on my slippers—a present from Santa *last* year—and headed down the stairs. For the first time ever I was not going to be dragging Mom out of bed on Christmas morning.

My grogginess gave way to anticipation, and my heart began to race. Visions of my new bike consumed me. I knew that since I had made a promise to God to earn it, this would be the year that I would finally get exactly what I deserved. I'd waited patiently for so long, watching as every one of my friends had gotten the bike they'd asked for. Now it was my turn. Mom was right, His arms were around me, and after all I'd been through they were about to deliver the one present that could make me happy again.

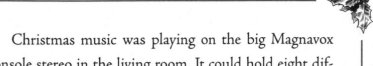

Christmas music was playing on the big Magnavox console stereo in the living room. It could hold eight different albums. When one was over, the tone arm would come up and the next album would fall onto the turntable. That morning all the albums were from the Firestone Christmas series. I think we got them one year when we bought our tires.

As I rounded the corner into the living room, I heard Julie Andrews and my mom singing together. "They know that Santa's on his way, he's loaded lots of toys and goodies on his sleigh."

65

"Merry Christmas, Eddie!" I'd been spotted. Mom danced around the corner from the kitchen. She wiped her hands on her apron and held them out as an invitation to a Christmas hug.

"Merry Christmas, Mom," I said as I gave her a twelve-year-old half-a-hug. I didn't want to get pancake flour all over my pajamas, and I knew that if I let her give me a full hug it would be five minutes before I wriggled out of it.

I broke free as quickly as I could and headed toward the tree in the corner. It glowed with a single strand of lights that were too big for the small evergreen. Popcorn strings and foil icicles connected ornaments of glass, wood, and paper. Very few of the ornaments were store bought. Many were the result of school projects or family activities, but most had been made by Mom over the years.

I moved my practiced gaze around the green felt skirt at the base of the tree where Mom had stitched the nativity scene. There were only a couple of gifts that hadn't been there on Christmas Eve and only one that I didn't immediately recognize from Operation Sneak Preview. None of them were even close to being large enough to be a bike, but I still had high hopes. I knew that Mom had enough of Grandpa in her blood to put me through the same kind of cat-and-mouse games that he did. A few years ago she'd waited until all of my presents had been opened before pointing through the back window to my last present: a brand-new sled with a big bow on top.

With that Christmas still fresh in my head, I began to think how Mom might have hidden the bike. There were a lot of possibilities, but my guess was that she'd probably wrapped up a picture of the Huffy and stashed the actual bike in the garage. It would fit her perfectly—she could keep me guessing while not wasting any wrapping paper, something she always seemed to be preoccupied with.

I picked up a present so that I could better see what was behind it, hoping to find one that I hadn't yet seen so I could shake it.

"Is that for me?" Mom sang.

She was too quick for me. "Oh, yes, Merry Christmas." I turned hesitantly from the gifts and handed her the present I'd paid for by picking berries at my grandfather's farm over the summer.

She carefully opened the clumsily wrapped package. "Gloves!" she exclaimed with a little too much enthusiasm for me to believe her. Then she got a thoughtful look on her face and said quietly, "I did need new gloves. They're perfect, honey. Thank you."

I wasn't listening, because I was too busy fishing for her other gift. I found it and handed it over. "Here's my other present for you."

"Oh, my, another one?" she said as she took the small, rectangular box. Inside were a handwritten card and a bar

67

of chocolate. " 'Merry Christmas, Mother,' " she read aloud. " 'You are as sweet as this chocolate.' " She laughed. "Eddie, did you buy this yourself?"

"Yes," I replied proudly. "I was thinking you could eat it or make cookies with it."

"Do you know what Baker's chocolate is?"

"It's chocolate you can bake, isn't it?" I replied. Mom smiled at the thought of how much I loved cookies yet obviously hadn't listened to a word my father had said about making them.

"Yes, dear, but it isn't very—" She stopped and smiled as if it had absolutely been the best Christmas gift she'd ever received. "You, *you* are the sweetest boy—I mean, young man—who ever lived." Then she opened the package and ate a square with her eyes squinting a bit and a grin on her face. "Best chocolate I've ever had."

She came to me and took me in her arms. It seemed like an eternity.

"My turn?" I asked anxiously.

"Your turn, sweetheart."

I first opened the presents that I had, well, already

opened. I did my best to act surprised as I held each of them up to show Mom: Homemade mittens from my cousin, a baseball from an uncle I hadn't seen in years, and a bag of candy that I was sure was the exact same striped stuff that I didn't eat the year before. I wondered if Mom hadn't been putting out the same bag every year since I was four.

Finally. Only one present was left. It was a fairly large box, but very light. *Please, God,* I thought to myself, *let it be a Polaroid or even a handwritten note or card.* I couldn't believe I was actually hoping to *not* open a BB gun or a set of walkie-talkies, but the Huffy was the only present on my mind. It was the only present that would make me happy.

Mom had decorated the box with a large bow and a ribbon that looked suspiciously like the one I'd taken off my birthday gift. I tore through reindeer-and-snowflakes wrapping paper until I was left with a simple plain brown box. My heart raced as I slowly lifted off the top and pushed aside the crinkled white tissue paper.

It was a sweater.

"Do you like it?" Mom asked as I stared at the gift, un-

69

able to speak. She shifted on the couch and crossed her arms as she waited several seconds for an answer.

Holding on to my last possible fragment of hope, I unfolded the sweater, hoping there was something tucked inside that would point me toward the bike. I shook it back and forth as hard as I could without being obvious, but nothing happened. That's when I realized there wouldn't be a bike that year—just a stupid, handmade, ugly sweater.

"Do you like it? Do you really like it?" Mom was hoping my silence was due to my unspeakable joy.

A stupid, handmade, ugly sweater that wasn't a bike.

"Sure, Mom, it's great." I felt like I should cry. I was entitled to cry, I thought, but it was the kind of sad that didn't include tears. If I hadn't worked so hard all year, if I hadn't thought about a new bike every waking second of my life, if I hadn't promised God I would *earn* it, then I might not have noticed how the color of the yarn would perfectly match the Wonder Bread polka dots on my bread-bag boots. But I had done all of those things, and I did notice.

"I'm really sorry about the bike, honey." Mom's voice was too soft and tender for how I felt. "It's just that the repairs for the roof were so much more than I expected. I know you understand. Maybe I can save up enough to get it for you next year."

I understood all right. I understood that we would always be the poor family and I would always be the poor kid with plastic boots and no bike.

I stared down at the sweater and felt my body temperature rise, almost as if I'd already put it on. I didn't know who had let me down more: Mom, for not buying me what I deserved; Dad, for not watching over me like he was supposed to; or God, for ignoring my promise. I was so disappointed with all of them that I forgot I was supposed to put the neck under my chin as if I'd been trying it on.

"I hope it fits!" Mom said, trying to remind me to do the "chin thing." I didn't get the hint.

"I'm sure it will," I replied without enthusiasm. Mom finally came over, took the sweater from me, and held it up to my back. She pressed her fingers into my shoulders as

71

she matched the edges to the outline of my body. "Oh sure," she said. "At the rate you're growing it will be just the right size by next fall!" She was way too excited about the whole thing.

I could muster only a halfhearted reply. "Thanks, Mom, it's great."

"It's just like the expensive ones we sell at Sears," she offered proudly, attempting to combat the obvious disappointment that had involuntarily spread across my face. "We ask almost forty dollars for a real, hand-knit wool sweater. I couldn't afford that, of course, but I was able to come up with enough to buy the good yarn." She stopped talking and looked at me as if embarrassed to be explaining her gift.

72

"Really, it's great. Really. I did need a sweater." I couldn't get past my own disappointment or look beyond myself to see what the gift meant to her.

I thought back to the note Mom had left for me under her bed. She was right, I had "missed" my gift. Mom had been making it right in front of me every night while forcing me to watch *Little House on the Prairie.* (She thought Pa

Ingalls was cute, and I had to suffer for it.) But now it all made sense: a stupid handmade gift made while watching a stupid show. I bet my friends who got to watch the shows they wanted, like *Starsky and Hutch*, also got presents they'd actually asked for.

My disappointment over the morning snow now seemed trivial compared to how upset I was about my present. *You're an idiot*, I thought to myself. *You should have known. You should have seen it coming.*

Mom looked at me with eyes that were, for once, surprisingly hard to read. Was she relieved that I seemed to be so happy, or did she see right through my act? Quite honestly, at that moment, I didn't really care, but I knew that I couldn't keep up the charade forever. I had to escape.

73

"I'm just going to run up to my bedroom and put it away. I'll be back in a few minutes." I felt a familiar, relentless burn returning to my eyes. I ran upstairs before Mom could see my tears.

Five

y bedroom window looked out over the
street in front of our house. Before my
prepubescent growth spurt, I could stand at the sill, put
my elbows on it, and rest my chin on my hands.

That Christmas morning I was just a little too tall to
do that anymore, so I stood back a few inches, put my
hands on the sill, and leaned forward until my forehead
rested against the cold glass. It burned my skin, but I felt
like I deserved the pain.

The snow had finally started. They were big, beautiful
flakes, and the thin white coating on the street meant that

it had already been falling for a while now. I guess I'd been too busy feeling sorry for myself to notice.

I was just about to turn away when I saw the little girl across the street riding a brand-new bike in her driveway. Her dad was walking alongside, as if he didn't trust the training wheels on the slippery asphalt. My eyes began to burn again, right along with my forehead.

I crossed over to my bed and fell on it. Luke Skywalker taunted me with the memory of a great Christmas present from the past. Images of the girl on the bike kept running through my head. I saw the wheels spin around and around as she rode it like she'd been the freest girl in the world. Free to travel two, three, maybe four houses away. *Free.*

I focused on my ceiling. It was filthy. The roof leaked a little every time it rained, and water soaked the plaster, leaving splotches and lines. Nothing in my life was perfect. Other kids had new bikes, two parents, *and* ceilings that didn't leak. It just wasn't fair.

"Eddie!" Mom cried out from the hall as my bedroom door swung open. "Have you looked outside yet? Dad's gift to you is here . . . it's a Christmas miracle! It hasn't snowed like this since—"

I had been staring at the ceiling, unable to look at her when she came in. I knew my face would betray me. But after a few seconds of silence I sat up on the bed to see what was going on. Mom was staring at the floor by my dresser. "Is that your sweater?" she asked quietly. I had dropped it there without even thinking. It was rolled up like a ball, like something that belonged in the trash can.

"Sorry. I should have put it away," I said meekly as I started to get up from the bed.

"It looks like you already have," she replied. The pain in her voice and the disappointment on her face shouldn't have surprised me, but it did. After a few moments of silence, she looked up from the sweater and directly into my eyes. "Please don't treat your sweater that way."

I knew that we didn't have much money, but until that moment I never realized how heavily that weighed on my mother. In my mind I saw my mom walking by the new bikes in Sears every day at work, knowing which one I

77

wanted and knowing she couldn't afford it. I saw her looking at the sweaters I didn't want, and she couldn't afford, picking out yarn and knitting every night while trying to convince herself that somehow I would understand and love that sweater just as much as a new bike. Knowing in her heart I never could.

I sat there awkwardly, watching in silence as Mom picked up the sweater as gently as if it had been an injured kitten. She slowly folded it and neatly placed it on top of my dresser. She lingered there for a moment, her hands pressing the sweater down as if to flatten out wrinkles that didn't exist.

I really didn't know how much my mother believed in the magic of Christmas until I saw it die for her in a rumpled ball on my bedroom floor.

Mom gently pulled my bedroom door closed without another word. My eyes began to burn again. I went back to the window, hoping the snow would cheer me up. I pressed my head up against the cold glass again. The girl across the street was gone, and so was the snow. One final flurry danced slowly toward the ground. It looked as sad and alone as I felt.

Then it started to rain.

When Dad first started to get sick, Mom, along with some of our close family friends, tried to keep City Bakery going. They did the best they could, but it quickly became obvious just how good a baker Dad really was. A recipe might seem like a simple list of ingredients and instructions, but there was obviously a lot more that went into his creations than just what was handwritten on a bunch of old grease-stained pages.

When Dad passed away, Mom quickly sold the business. I guess it was probably inevitable anyway. Our downtown, like my father, had been slowly dying for years. I don't know how much money she got, but I do know that it couldn't have been much, because even after she got the check I still wasn't allowed to order milk when we went out to eat. I think she used most of it to pay off Dad's medical bills.

I never thought I'd miss the bakery, but the truth was that I did. I missed it a lot. I didn't miss cleaning the pans or sweeping the floor, but I missed being together. Even though we'd all been working, we'd all been working *together*. Somehow that had escaped me until it was gone.

For a long time, Mom avoided driving by the bakery after she sold it, but someone told me it had been turned into a shoe store. I took their word for it; it was too hard to picture someone trying on a pair of high heels in the same place my father used to crack eggs or knead dough.

Right around the time Mom sold the bakery, she also sold our car and house. I guess she was trying to make a clean break. The Impala got traded in for our Pinto wagon, and our house was downsized to a white one so small that our one-car garage basically doubled the size of the whole interior.

I didn't like all of the new stuff, but at least the Pinto didn't have the smell of Dad's Old Spice cologne trapped in the fabric of its headrests, and the new house didn't constantly smell like Dad's German chocolate cake.

Thinking about all the changes that had happened so

quickly in my life only added to my misery. If Dad had still been alive and still had the bakery, then he would've had enough money to buy my bike. It just wasn't fair. Why was I being punished?

After about an hour of watching the rain I went back downstairs. Mom was in the kitchen. "Is there anything left for lunch?" I asked, hoping that we could pretend the sweater incident had never happened.

"We don't have time now. We're going to head over to Grandma and Grandpa's house a little early. Go put on your sweater—your grandmother helped me pick out the yarn and pattern, and she's very excited to see you in it." She spoke without any joy. Like me, she had apparently decided to pretend that the sweater incident had never happened.

With the way things were going, I did *not* want to go to my grandparents' farm, and I definitely did *not* want to wear what I was sure was an itchy, hot, uncomfortable, not-a-bicycle sweater.

I went back upstairs and put on the sweater. The full-length mirror hanging on the back of my door caught my

81

attention. I stared into my own eyes. What was I doing? I looked at myself in the sweater that I knew my mother had worked so hard on and was so proud of. I wanted to like it, but I couldn't.

I left my bedroom, slammed the door shut, and not too quietly stormed around the house. Remembering the lessons from my grandfather, I tried to create just enough of a ruckus to make a point, but not so much as to get into trouble.

It didn't work.

Mom handed me two bread bags and glared at me with eyes that I dared not try to read. It never dawned on me that Mom knew her father's tricks far better than I ever would.

Six

'm only going to say this once, Edward Lee. When we get to the farm, you will be a boy having a merry Christmas. Is that clear?"

Mom using my full first name was always a bad sign, but Mom using my full first name *and* my middle name was almost unprecedented. This was a code-red alert.

"Clear," I answered curtly as I stared out the back window of our Pinto. I could never figure out why Mom would spend as much time driving to see my grandparents as we actually spent visiting with them. The drive was an hour and a half each way and we rarely stayed much longer than two hours unless we were sleeping over.

Except for the sound of heavy rain battering the roof and spraying up from the tires, the ride was spent mostly in silence. Mom stared straight ahead. She didn't even look at me in the mirror.

The radio was playing a Christmas song by the Carpenters, but it felt as out of place as if it had been July. Mom reached over and rolled the front passenger window down partway, letting cold, wet air rush into the car. The Pinto's heater only had two settings: Off and Furnace. I didn't know if she was getting sleepy or if she was just taking pity on me in my heavy wool sweater.

86

As we drove, the houses got further and further apart, until finally I saw the first in a series of small farms that lined my grandparents' street. One of them was obviously vacant. There were big gaps in the wooden fencing, an overgrown front lawn, and an old farmhouse that looked empty and unsteady. I thought I saw a flash of light in one of its broken windows.

No. It must be a reflection. Who would live in a place like that?

Less than a minute later, I saw Grandma's hydrangea bushes and the old plow that Grandpa had put at the end of the drive to mark his small raspberry and chicken farm. Mom turned in, and the sound of our tires crunching through the wet gravel floated in through the window.

The Pinto's engine always ran for a couple of seconds every time it was shut off. I usually made a game of getting out of the car before the rumbling stopped, but this time I waited for Mom to get out before I reluctantly followed her.

"Merry Christmas, Mary!"

"Merry Christmas, Mom," she answered. Her voice seemed to have softened a little since she'd last spoken to me.

"Merry Christmas, Mr. Eddie," Grandpa teased. He laughed whenever he called me that. I didn't understand why until Mom sat me down in front of a rerun of an old show with a guy who talked to his horse. But did Wilbur ever call Mr. Ed "Mr. Eddie"? I don't think so.

"Hi, Grandpa," I mumbled. I was trying hard to maintain my sour attitude, but he always made that hard.

87

"Look at that *beautiful* sweater," Grandma said as she took me by the shoulders. Luckily, she wasn't a cheek-pincher. "And such fine knitting." She gave my mother a quick look of approval. "How do you like it, Eddie?"

I looked over at Mom. She was watching me, expressionless, waiting to see what I was going to say. After quickly considering all possible answers, I said, "It's fine. Maybe a little scratchy . . . or itchy . . . or whatever. But it's fine. I like it."

Mom's icy stare made the short walk to the front door seem like a mile. Her eyes were lecturing me again.

My grandfather was a big man with snow-colored hair. It was more white than gray, but not like an old person's. For years I thought he was Santa. He and Grandma were the same age, but she had beautiful brown hair with just a hint of gray in it. "A miracle of modern science," Grandpa liked to say.

I sat on the big, old, comfortable sofa in front of the fire, and Grandpa sat across from me in his chair while Mom and Grandma worked in the kitchen. Grandpa didn't know it, but Mom and I called it his "storytelling chair," because he couldn't seem to sit in it without offering some epic tale from his past. The problem was that Grandpa was so good at mixing fact with fiction that almost no one, including him, was really sure what was true anymore. Asking him to retell a story only made things worse. "Grandpa," I once asked, hoping he'd confirm a story I'd remembered from years earlier, "did you really help build the lunar rover?"

He loved to answer a question with a question. "Have I ever lied to you?" he replied, making sure that if he had told the story "in fun," he wasn't going to lie now by confirming it. It was the perfect system. Even Grandma didn't seem to know the truth anymore. When I would ask her to confirm one of Grandpa's tales, she would simply say, "Could be." She wasn't being coy or playing along, she really just didn't know anymore. "Could be . . ." was the best—no, make that the *only*—answer she could legitimately give.

Sometimes Grandpa would begin weaving a story together and, after a few sentences, Grandma would show her disapproval by yelling his name: "Edward!" Grandpa would then lower his voice and tell me to move closer to his chair. The procedure would repeat itself throughout the story until finally I would be sitting at my grandfather's feet, looking up at him in awe as he whispered lie after lie.

"Grandpa, did you really build this whole house by yourself?"

"Yes, in fact, without a hammer and with only two—"

"EDWARRRRRRD!" Grandma yelled from the

90

kitchen. I never knew how she could hear him from that far away. Mom always used to tell me that she had eyes in the back of her head, so I guess I just figured that Grandma had ears in other rooms.

Now, as my grandfather sat across from me in his chair, stroking his chin on a rainy Christmas afternoon, I hoped that he would start in on another story. I couldn't have cared less if he made the whole thing up; I just didn't want to think about the sweater, bikes, or Dad anymore.

Unfortunately, he had another idea. "So, Eddie, are you ready to try and beat me at Chinese checkers?"

Chinese checkers? What the heck was going on? I figured that Grandpa had either taken every last dime from the people he played cards with or he was looking to test his system out on a different game. I risked pressing the issue. "Why don't you want to play cards?"

"Cards?" Grandpa looked away quickly, a telltale sign that he was about to make something up. "I haven't been able to find my deck. Besides, Chinese checkers is more fun. You don't have to do any math."

Math? Apparently Grandpa's system was even more complicated than I thought. But at that point the truth was that no game sounded like very much fun. "No thanks, Grandpa."

"Something wrong, Eddie?"

"Nah, it just doesn't feel like Christmas. Maybe it's the rain."

"Hmmm. Not Christmas? I'd better get rid of that tree, then," he said with a smile much warmer than I deserved.

I was thinking about telling him what had happened that morning, how I'd gotten a sweater instead of the bike

91

that I deserved. If anyone would understand my disappointment, it was Grandpa. I figured if that went well, maybe I would apologize to Mom for the way I'd acted. The ninety minutes of silence in the car ride over had made the trip seem so long that the thought of enduring an equally silent ride home was almost unbearable.

I was about to tell Grandpa the story when I caught sight of their Christmas tree. It was unlike me to not have already noticed it and done a thorough investigation. There were only a few presents under it.

Grandpa caught me looking. "You know Grandma doesn't put them there."

I was lost in thought, and I barely heard what Grandpa had said. I turned back to face him. "What?"

"Grandma. She thinks that you and I take sneak peeks at the presents, so she won't put them under the tree anymore. She hides them."

"Why would she think that?" A slight smile involuntarily took hold of my face. I wasn't as experienced at lying as Grandpa was.

"I have no idea." Grandpa's face gave nothing away.

"But I do know this: If pirates hid their treasure the way Grandma hides her presents, they'd have all gone bankrupt. I'm getting socks and a new tool belt."

I don't know why I was surprised, but I was. "What about me? What am I getting?"

"Oh, I don't know, Eddie. I do know that you have some pajamas coming, but she hasn't even wrapped them. I think she's just going to put them in your dresser." Grandpa looked away. "But other than that I couldn't find any of yours. Say, would you mind helping me bring in some more firewood?"

93

"No, I don't mind." It was really hard to say no to my grandfather and impossible to do it twice in a row.

We trudged through what was left of a sloppy, wet snow to a long stack of firewood. I caught myself enjoying my attempts to completely hide my footprints inside my grandfather's. It wasn't hard; his feet seemed to be about three times bigger than mine.

"Grandpa," I whispered, "what do you mean you couldn't find my presents?"

Grandpa ignored my question as he piled sticks of

wood into my cradled arms, making sure to add one more than I could comfortably carry. He tucked a single piece under his arm, stuck his hands in his coat pockets, and followed me back to the house.

"*There* you are," Grandma said as she opened the door for me. "We were beginning to think you two got lost."

Grandma knew better than anyone that Grandpa *never* got lost. Sure, he usually wasn't where everyone else thought he should be, but Grandpa always knew where he was and, more importantly, why he was there.

Grandpa winked at me. "What do you mean, dear? Eddie and I were just getting some wood."

"I thought maybe you'd gone into town without telling us," she said with a smile.

Whenever I'd visit, Grandpa looked for any excuse to take me into town. He could turn the simplest errand into an adventure in finding the gray area between the letter and spirit of Grandma's law. A few summers earlier, Grandma asked him to go to the hardware store to pick up some new bags for the vacuum cleaner, and I tagged along. Instead of going to the one that was about ten minutes away, Grandpa drove us all the way to the far end of town to another hardware store. It didn't take long for me to figure out why: This particular store happened to have a soft-serve ice cream counter in the back.

We got back three hours later. Grandma didn't even have to ask what happened; our ice cream mustaches gave us away. But before she could say a word, Grandpa pulled the vacuum bags out and gave her a big hug. It was really hard for anyone ever to be mad at him.

A smile crept across my face as I thought about that trip.

Mom was standing behind Grandma, wearing one of her gingham aprons. She saw me smile, and she smiled back.

As only a twelve-year-old could, I stupidly put up another wall and acted as though I wasn't ready to give in yet.

I looked right past her.

If Grandpa was the king of telling stories, the dinner table was his court. It was always fun, but since Grandma made us wait to open our presents until after dinner, Grandpa tried to keep his stories shorter than usual on Christmas. He wanted to get to the tree just as much as I did.

This year Grandpa seemed to be in an exceptional hurry. Mom and I knew he was up to something, but neither of us could figure out what it was. Finally, about halfway through dinner, Grandma apparently had had enough of his fidgeting. She turned to him and whispered, "Tomorrow, Edward." Grandpa's face revealed his disappointment.

96

After the coffee was poured we all filed into the family room. Grandpa sat in his storytelling chair, Mom and Grandma sat on the couch. I went right to the tree. I was given the Santa hat; as usual, I was the designated present distributor. I got right to work.

"Here you go, Grandpa," I said as I brought him a present that was suspiciously light. *Light as socks*, I thought to myself. Grandpa winked at me as I put the box by his feet.

Each time I went back to retrieve another box from under the tree I secretly hoped to find my name written on the tag—but it happened only twice. Even Mom had three presents.

I slowly started to unwrap my first gift when I noticed that the piece of tape sealing one of the end flaps had a slight bubble in it. Grandpa. I looked up to give him my version of the "I know what you did" look, but he ignored my glare and concentrated intently on his present.

Given the size of my two presents, I knew that neither would contain a bike, but I still held out hope—just as I had before opening my sweater earlier that morning. *What if Grandpa wrapped up a picture of a bike?* I would never put anything past Grandpa's imagination, but I had to admit that it seemed like a stretch at this point.

"Socks!" My thoughts were interrupted by Grandpa's overly excited scream from across the room. Gosh, he was good at this.

While most people on television tear off the wrapping paper, crinkle it up into a ball, and throw it into the trash bag across the room, we always had to open the packages slowly and carefully so that we could reuse the paper the following year. I think my mom and grandmother were

97

secretly in a game to see which one of them would be the first to be unable to salvage the paper anymore. This year each of their gifts had been wrapped in paper that was only two years younger than I was.

While I always hated the whole paper-saving process because it slowed down the present opening, it did help cover up any mistakes that Grandpa and I might've made during our "previews." If we'd accidentally torn a bit of paper or ripped a piece of tape, it could always be blamed on the mandatory recycling program.

98

I picked up one of the boxes that had my name on it. It wasn't even wrapped. I slowly pulled the ribbon off, lifted the top, and pushed the tissue paper out of the way. My heart was racing with anticipation. If anyone would wrap up a clue to a scavenger hunt that would end with a bike, it was my grandfather.

My hands shook with excitement. I looked up at Grandpa, and he had a wide, twelve-year-old's smile on his face. It was a good sign.

I tore through the final piece of tissue paper and finally uncovered the gift: Handmade pajamas and a pair of handmade slippers that were made with the same yarn as my sweater.

Fantastic. I'd been fooled again.

Not wanting a repeat of the sweater incident, I put on the happiest expression I could muster. "Thanks, Grandma, these are really nice. They match my sweater perfectly." By now I was getting pretty good at faking excitement.

"They certainly should . . . your mother and I split the yarn. What a deal we got!"

"A tool belt!" I heard Grandpa bellow from across the room. "What a surprise. It's exactly what I needed!"

The day was turning out to be a disaster, and I didn't want to drag it out any longer. I reached for my last present, feeling a little bit like Charlie Bucket opening the one Wonka bar my parents could afford, hoping to see a flash of gold but knowing the odds were against me.

I looked down at the tag and my heart sank. It was from my great-aunt, but "great" wasn't a word anyone would ever use to describe her gifts. She was as insane as she was old, and her presents were almost always something that she took directly out of her house and wrapped up. One year she gave me something that no one could identify. Grandpa swore it was an ashtray that he'd seen in her kitchen, but Mom thought it was an old homemade coffee mug. Either way, it was nothing I wanted. It now sat on top of my dresser at home, holding a nickel, a home-made pet rock, and a safety pin.

As I opened this year's gift, I prayed that it was something I could actually use. I wasn't disappointed; it was a roll of pennies.

You've got to be kidding me, I thought. *At least I know where to keep them.*

The rain was now beating down loudly on the roof of the farmhouse, and I could hear every drop echo, as if they'd all been falling in slow motion. All traces of snow and Christmas magic were now gathered in muddy brown puddles. I wished that I could start the day over again as a completely different person.

"Eddie, Grandma invited us to sleep over!" Mom interrupted my daydream. "We can have a big breakfast in the morning and drive home at lunchtime tomorrow."

I felt my heart rate quicken. I always loved sleeping

over at the farm. Grandpa and I would get into all kinds of trouble once Mom and Grandma were asleep. One time he and I spent two hours mixing up Grandma's kitchen spices by pouring each of them into a different bottle. Cinnamon became paprika. Parsley became dill. Dill became nutmeg. Nutmeg became rosemary. The next day's French toast was disgusting, but Grandpa and I laughed through every dill-filled bite that Grandma insisted we take.

The truth was that I really did want to stay over that night. I thought Grandpa might be the only person on earth who could make me forget about the day I'd had. But the twelve-year-old in me also didn't want to make it too easy on Mom after what *she'd* put me through. A sweater? Pajamas? A roll of pennies? It was the worst Christmas ever. I turned, gave my mother the best scowl I could muster, and said, "I really don't feel well. I just want to go home."

Grandpa looked at me quizzically.

My mother rubbed her forehead. "Eddie, I didn't sleep much last night, and you know I've been working longer shifts at the store. I'm exhausted and don't feel like driv-

101

ing." She cocked her head slightly and gave me a wink that spoke volumes. "Please, for me?"

I dug my heels in. "I really just want to get home. I'm sure some of my friends got presents that I'd like to play with." The look on Mom's face told me that I'd hit my mark. Grandpa's eyes narrowed, and I could feel the burn of his stare on the side of my face.

"I'm sorry, Eddie," Mom responded firmly. "We're staying. I'm just too tired to drive."

"It would mean a lot to us to have our two favorite people here for breakfast tomorrow," my grandmother interjected, trying to restore the peace.

Then Grandpa spoke up, his tone far more serious than I was used to. "I think Eddie's right. Maybe you two should just head home. After all, Eddie doesn't feel well."

I should've known that Grandpa would be onto my game. He thought more like a twelve-year-old than I did.

I tried to dig my way out of the mess by thinking one step ahead of him. "Actually, Grandpa, maybe Mom is right. Maybe we should stay. Don't you have some errands in town I could help out with in the morning?" I looked at

Grandpa with a wry smile, waiting for him to reciprocate. He didn't.

"No, nothing I can't take care of next week. I really think you guys should head home. I'm sure you can't wait to play with all your friends' great presents."

Checkmate. I looked down, embarrassed and angry.

My mother sighed. "Well, I guess that's that." Her eyes revealed both exhaustion and resignation. "Go upstairs and get your stuff packed up, Eddie. I need to talk to Grandma and Grandpa. I'll call you when I'm ready to go."

"Sure," I said, pretending not to be bothered by any of this.

"And put on your bread bags."

103

I jogged up the stairs. Punishing my mom had escalated further than I'd planned, and the look in her eyes hurt my heart. I washed over my guilt with anger. Anger at God, life, and, by association, my mother. *It's not my fault*, I told myself.

When I reached the bedroom, I took the bread bags out but didn't put them on. *Stupid boots.* I threw them onto the floor. What a stinking, lousy, crummy day. I hated

Christmas. I just wished it was over. But it wasn't even close to over—I still had what was sure to be a long, painfully silent drive ahead.

I took off my Christmas sweater and clutched it tightly in my arms as I lay down on the bed. *What a gift*, I thought sarcastically to myself. *What a perfect gift*. My eyes began to burn under the weight of my anger. I buried my head under the pillow, hoping that my mother wouldn't call for me until my tears had dried.

104

"Eddie," my mother's voice rang up the stairs, "it's time to go."

I groaned with exhaustion. I reluctantly put on my sweater, then lifted my bag and walked downstairs. Grandma had her arm around my mother's waist and was giving her a reassuring squeeze. "Don't forget to call me when you get home, Mary. I don't want to be up all night worrying."

For as long as I could remember, my mother would call my grandparents as soon as we returned home from their house. Since long-distance calls were a luxury for us, they had, with Grandpa's assistance, developed a system. Mom would use the operator to make a person-to-person call and ask for herself. Grandma would answer, claim her daughter had just left, and then hang up, knowing that her daughter had made it home safely. It was a great system . . . and, as Grandpa always stressed, "It was completely free and *almost* honest."

My grandparents went into the kitchen to box up the food we would have eaten together for breakfast. I could hear deliberately muffled conversation.

105

The stakes had just been raised, and I was going to win this mind game. No matter what it took.

Seven

e were twenty minutes into our drive home before either of us spoke. "You really outdid yourself this time, Eddie."

I watched a seemingly endless number of farms fade away in the rearview mirror. The clouds marking the edge of a winter storm had squeezed the sun into a sad, pale yellow circle with a gray halo.

"What do you want me to do?" Mom asked, trying to hide her tears.

"I want to have a real life." The words exploded from

my mouth. "Like my friends." I couldn't help it. A whole day of pent-up frustration and anger poured out.

"A real life? Eddie, this is the reality of my life. I work four different jobs. I feel like I haven't slept for two years. I switch hours with people so I can be home with you as much as possible. I can only do so much, Eddie. I'm tired. I'm so tired. And you know what else? Maybe it is time you start being the man you need to grow into, rather than acting like the eight-year-old kid you were."

I'd never heard my mother talk to me like that before. I looked up just in time to see her discreetly wipe a tear from her eye. When she spoke again, her tone was much softer.

"I know that things have been hard since Dad died. But it's been hard for both of us. At some point you have to realize that everything happens for a reason. It is up to you to find that reason, learn from it, and let it take you to the place you're supposed to be—not just where you have ended up." Mom spoke slowly. "You can either complain about how hard your life is, or you can realize that only you are responsible for it. You get to choose: Am I going to

108

be happy or miserable? And *nothing*—not a sweater, and certainly not a bike—will ever change that."

Something deep inside of me wanted to apologize and beg for my mother's forgiveness. Instead, I just sat there.

The day's steady rain had slowed to a drizzle, but the mist kicked up by the tires made it hard to see anything out the side window. Looking straight ahead was out of the question—Mom's eyes might be waiting in the mirror for another lecture—so I rolled my window down halfway and prayed we would just get home fast.

After a few minutes Grandma's church came into view 109 through the mist. I say "Grandma's church" because she was, by far, the most religious person in the family. Mom was in second place, but there was really no contest after that; Grandpa and I were tied for last.

When I was a little kid, I used to get dressed up and go to church with Mom every Sunday. I hated it. She made me sit up straight and "listen" for a whole hour. Dad never came with us; he usually just stayed at home or went golfing instead. He used to say he was a big believer in *all* of the Ten Commandments, especially the one that mandated "rest on the Sabbath." Mom often reminded him that golf was probably not what the Lord had in mind, but Dad would just laugh and say, "God doesn't take attendance on Sunday." A part of me thought he was just saying that to make himself feel better about not going with us, but when I saw the way Dad treated others and cared for those in need, I understood what he really meant: God takes attendance *every* day.

During the summer, when I'd stay over at my grandparents' house a lot, we would go to Grandma's church every Sunday. It was the only time I ever actually looked forward to going, because Grandpa and I used to make up games to pass the time. We came up with a whole bunch of them over the years, but my favorite was a game we called Stand for God. (Grandpa originally tried to call it Jump for Jesus, but even he knew that was over the line, so we settled on the safer name.)

The rules were simple: Each time the service called for the congregation to sit, stand, kneel, or sing, you had to be first. It probably sounds easy, but to win you had to guess really early. If you guessed wrong, you not only lost but you also looked like an idiot—and got a full dose of Grandma's evil eye. Now that I think back, it's pretty obvious where Mom learned her uncanny ability to lecture with her eyes.

The more we played Stand for God, the better Grandpa and I got at it, and the earlier you had to guess if you wanted to win. One time Grandpa started singing "On Eagle's Wings" so early that Father Sullivan actually stopped reading the scripture and glared at him from the pulpit. Not coincidentally, that was also the last time Grandpa and I ever got to sit next to each other.

After Grandma started sitting between us, the masses seemed to take forever, but, over time, something strange began to happen: I started to actually enjoy them. I think part of it was that I felt closest to Dad when I was there. It's hard to describe, but there were times when I'd feel him sitting right there next to me. Sometimes I even heard his horrible voice singing right along with mine.

As I looked out the back windshield, Grandma's church, the place where I felt the most connected to my father, was now just a dot in the fog. I thought how strange

111

it was that a person sitting just two feet away from me felt more distant than someone who wasn't even alive.

With the church now beyond the horizon, I turned back around and risked a quick glance up front. Mom's eyes were waiting for me in the mirror—but they weren't angry or hurt anymore, they were just tired. I knew that she was giving me an opening to apologize and all would be forgotten. But I still wasn't ready. I was tired too.

About ten minutes later, I fell asleep.

So did Mom.

112

I woke to the ticking sound the Ford's engine made while it cooled. I looked up and saw the seat I'd just been sitting in. A mix of twisted metal and wires came at me from all angles, like angry, bony fingers. Shredded fabric from Mom's headrest hung down. Something on the dashboard was blinking and lighting up a tiny spot on the floor every few seconds.

A pair of strong, weathered hands reached in and

pulled me through the partially opened, upside-down back door. I didn't see the man's face, but as he held me tight I noticed how filthy his hands were.

"Mom!" I tried to scream but nothing came out of my mouth. I was shivering inside my sweater.

I must have drifted off again, because when I awoke I was on the pavement about twenty yards from the now-burning car. Brilliant red and orange fingers reached up high into the eternal night sky. The heat was overwhelming. I heard the ominous echo of sirens and saw flashing lights reflect off of distant clouds.

113

I fell asleep again.

I opened my eyes to excruciatingly bright lights. Doctors and nurses buzzed all around, but none of them seemed to be paying much attention to me.

"Where's my mother?" I screamed. "How's my mother? I want to see my mother!"

The doctors only answered my questions with another question, just like Grandpa did whenever he was trying to avoid the truth: "How do we get in touch with your father?"

"My father is . . . dead," I remember whispering. Then I drifted off to sleep again.

Eight

hen I was ten years old my grandparents took me to the annual Puyallup Fair. It was no Disneyland, but after years of roller-skating on a level driveway for thrills, it was a welcome change. Grandma refused to go on any rides—she only liked the shows and the FFA exhibits—and Grandpa wouldn't go on anything that went in a circle because it made him sick. That didn't leave very many options; after the petting zoo, bobbing for apples, and a slow scenic train ride (that was still too fast for Grandma), I was ready for something bigger. I was ready for the roller coaster.

"The Coaster Thrill Ride," as it was officially known, must've been named by the engineer who'd built it. After all, what other explanation could there be for the best ride in the park having such a boring, generic name?

Originally built in 1935 out of Douglas fir, the Coaster Thrill Ride wasn't the biggest or fastest coaster in the country, but it still looked plenty scary to me. It had been destroyed by fire in the 1950s before being rebuilt, again out of wood, and it now towered over the fair as a beacon for thrill seekers everywhere.

As Grandpa and I stood in line, we wondered out loud which train car we'd get: Or'nry Orange, Blaz'n Blue, or Ol' Yeller. Grandpa talked a big game the whole time we waited. "Are you sure about this, Eddie?" he asked me. "It's a fifty-foot drop and hits over 50 miles an hour. I can handle it. Can you?"

"Sure," I told him, though truthfully I was anything but sure.

After finally making it to the station, we stepped into our car and lowered the safety bar across our laps. I glanced up at Grandpa one last time and swore I caught a glimpse of fear in his eyes.

The unmistakable clicking of the old wooden coaster's pull chain engaged, and soon we were heading up the first big hill. Neither Grandpa nor I said a word.

The view from the top was amazing. The car briefly paused, as if caught in gravity's web, and I swore I saw Grandma's church in the distance, its steeple clock reflecting the sun. I didn't have a chance to look for long. We crested the hill, picked up speed, and hurtled back toward the ground, the wooden track shaking violently beneath us. Grandpa squeezed my hand and told me not to be afraid.

I didn't realize until years later that he was actually holding my hand tighter than I was holding his.

Now, as Grandpa and I stood together at my mother's wake, he was once again squeezing my hand tight. I didn't know who was comforting whom, but it was the only thing that kept me from running out the door.

I found out later that Mom had fallen asleep at the wheel. We'd drifted off the road and flipped in a ditch. I didn't have a scratch on me, but Mom had broken her neck. Doctors and friends kept telling me that she had died instantly, that she hadn't felt any pain—like that somehow made it all okay, but it didn't. I wanted my mother back. She wasn't supposed to die. Not then, not now, and certainly not "instantly." I never said good-bye, but, more important, I never told her that I was sorry. Now she would never know.

"Oh, Eddie." Aunt Cathryn hugged me tight, her eyes swollen and red and her voice uncharacteristically soft. "I'm so sorry." She tried to keep talking, but her words didn't make any sense.

Mrs. Benson and the others from the nursing home were there as well. But there wasn't any cheek-pinching or caroling now, just tears and tender hugs. I wondered if I would ever see any of them again.

Grandma said it would upset me if I touched Mom's

hand, but I didn't care, I couldn't possibly be any more upset than I already was. I went up to her casket. She didn't seem real. She didn't look like my mother at all—she looked more like one of the mannequins she used to dress at Sears. So still. So peaceful. Her soft hand, which used to push the hair out of my eyes, now lay lifeless across her chest, clutching a rosary. She was wearing a dress I had never seen before and makeup I was sure she had never bought.

I reached out to touch her and noticed that I was wearing my Christmas sweater. I didn't even remember putting it on.

I wanted to cry. Actually, I felt like I *should* have cried, but as I stood there holding my mother's hand, I was surprised to find that all I felt was anger. I was angry at a lot of people, but no one more than God. He'd now taken both my father and my mother. Why? What had they ever done to deserve that? God could've saved them from disease and car wrecks, but he'd chosen not to. God could've answered my prayers, but instead he'd ignored them. God hadn't been there when my father had prayed for a second chance. He

121

hadn't been there when my mother had prayed for a blessed Christmas. And he obviously wasn't there now.

Grandpa must've sensed the transformation in my emotions. Just as I was about to collapse under the weight of all that I had been through and all that I still had to go through, he put his strong arms around me, pulled me close, and whispered three words that I didn't understand at the time but that have stayed with me ever since: *"All is well."*

But with everything I loved once again lying in a casket, he couldn't have been more wrong. Nothing was well. Nothing ever would be well again.

122

The months after my mother's death and funeral compressed themselves into a single point. I knew I was there, but my memories were like stories told by someone else. The fogginess lasted a long time. I didn't live the time after the accident so much as I watched it unfold.

I moved to my grandparents' farm. My room at their house looked a lot like my old one, except the water spot on the ceiling was gone and I could always hear the chickens in the morning and the cows in the afternoon through my bedroom window. Their house smelled like bacon and fresh bread twenty-four hours a day, scents that always reminded me where I was and why I was there.

I quickly became consumed with myself and what had happened to me. It was pretty easy to do. God obviously had it out for me, and now I had nothing but time to wonder why.

My old friends called in the beginning to see how I was doing, but being outside of bike-ride range made it tough to get together. Of course, I didn't have a bike, so that didn't really matter anyway.

Aunt Cathryn tried to call a few times as well, but it was awkward, because neither of us really knew how to talk to each other without Mom. Since long-distance calling was a luxury, it didn't take long for us to lose touch.

Grandpa and I still made trips into town to buy feed or wire or whatever was written on the scrap of paper tucked into his shirt pocket. He hadn't changed, but I had. My mood was dark. I was angry. After a few trips I quit

123

going voluntarily, and Grandpa stopped trying to make it fun. They became quick, silent, and all about getting what we were sent for and getting home as quickly as possible. After a few more trips like that, Grandpa quit dragging me along.

One trip that didn't stop was our weekly visit to Grandma's church. We never missed a service. But there were no more games to pass the time; Grandpa didn't want to be distracted. "Be respectful," he would gently whisper during the sermon, "I'm trying to listen. You should too."

After mass ended, Grandma and Grandpa would usually sit in the front pew by themselves, put their heads down, and pray. I would stand in the back and wait for them. Sometimes I'd try to rearrange the prayer candles to create a pattern; other times I'd play with the holy water— but mostly I was just bored. I didn't even feel close to Dad there anymore—it was like he and God had decided to abandon me at the same time.

After a few weekends of watching my grandparents fool themselves into thinking God would help, I made a decision: They could make me go to church, but they couldn't make me listen. Grandpa might have thought he could find answers at church, but I already had mine: *God was dead.* It wasn't that he didn't exist; he just didn't exist for *me.* He heard my prayers and decided to ignore them, so now I would ignore Him right back.

I would make Him suffer as much as He was making me.

With no trips into town, Grandpa quickly manufactured other opportunities to guide his wayward grandson. Good weather brought a change in chores, and he decided it was worth forcing me to help him.

Grandpa believed that hardware stores and lumberyards were only good for nails. After all, why pay for wood and windows when you could get them free from old barns or outbuildings? Grandpa had turned getting free supplies into a sport. Once he spotted a target, he would stop and ask the owner if he could relieve him of his broken-down eyesore. Usually the owner was so glad to have somebody haul the dilapidated building away that he'd jump at Grandpa's offer.

Once in a while someone would offer to sell him the

125

wood, but Grandpa would politely decline. He never, ever paid for something that he could get for free. In some cases, if the person trying to get him to pay had just moved from Seattle, or, worse, some big city in California, Grandpa would talk them into paying him to remove the free supplies. He said that it was good for them to learn how things worked "out here in the sticks with us yokels."

Grandpa kept all the spare wood and windows he collected behind his barn. It had all been stacked hastily over the years and was in serious disarray. One day he led me back there, showed me the pile, and told me that he and I were going to build a new chicken house. I wasn't exactly excited, but when he told me that all of the supplies first needed to be moved, stacked, and organized, I was downright angry. I couldn't believe it. It would take me forever.

Grandpa walked away for a few minutes and soon came back with two glasses of lemonade. He saw that I was struggling to move a large railroad tie, so he quickly put the glasses down and rushed over to my side to grab an end.

"Don't bother," I told him. "I've got it." I was so angry

126

that he was dumping all this work on my shoulders that I didn't even want him around me. Grandpa had never seen me like this before. Quite frankly, neither had I.

Grandpa backed off immediately, picked up his glass, took a sip, and stood there watching me for a few minutes. I didn't say a word. I didn't even look at him. I wanted him to know that while I was going to finish his stupid chore, I wasn't going to make him feel good about it. Finally, as he turned to leave he said simply, "Let me know when you're done, Eddie."

Every couple of hours or so Grandpa would peek around the back of the barn to see how I was doing or to bring me another lemonade from the house. Each time he would ask me the same question: "Eddie, are you done yet?"

As the days passed, Grandpa's visits didn't get any less frequent. He'd watch as I would struggle to lift and drag heavy beams from one part of the farm to another. He never even offered the obvious advice that it would have been wise to remove the old nails before moving the wood.

127

A few times I saw him sitting on the back porch, laughing as he told tall tales to our neighbor David. Another time I came around the corner to get a drink of water out of the hose and saw him sleeping in the hammock. The sound of the spigot being turned woke him up, and our eyes met. "Are you done yet?" he asked me. I was seething.

What a joke, I thought to myself. *Now I know why Grandpa is handling Mom's death so well. He's happy to have me at the farm because he finally has someone to do all the hard work, all of his work, for free.*

With an increasingly sore body, and hands covered in cuts and slivers, my rage grew every time Grandpa asked me if I was done yet. How could someone be so cold-hearted as to watch their own grandson struggle and never once even offer to help?

About four days into my task, Grandpa came out with more lemonade, looked me right in the eyes, and recited the same question he'd been asking all along: "Are you done yet?" I just about went crazy. "Are you kidding me?" I shouted back at him. "Look at this pile. It will be days before I can move all of this. If you're in such a hurry, maybe you could stop entertaining guests, taking naps, or trying to ease your conscience by bringing me stupid lemonade and offer to help me instead."

Grandpa looked at me sadly. "Eddie, I have offered to help you. I offered the first day, and I've offered every couple of hours since."

"When?" I shouted, bending down to continue my work. "All you've ever asked is when I'm gonna be done."

"No, Eddie, that may be what you've heard, but that's not what I've been asking." His voice was steady and calm. "I've been asking if *you* were done yet."

"Oh, sorry, Mr. English Professor." I had never been this disrespectful to my grandfather. I felt myself changing, and while that scared me, I wasn't sure how to stop it—and a growing part of me didn't even want to.

Grandpa grabbed me and, for the first and only time in my life, slapped me across the face. Tears welled up in his eyes.

He was quiet for a few moments as he collected himself. When he spoke again, his voice was soft. "When I

129

showed you all of this work the other day, I said 'we' were going to build a new chicken coop. I didn't say 'I,' and I certainly didn't say 'you.' I never intended for you to do all this work yourself. You just assumed it. When I offered to help, you told me 'not to bother.' If you remember correctly, that is the first time I asked you to let me know when you were done. I didn't mean done with the chore, I meant to let me know when you were done moping around. When are you going to be done feeling sorry for yourself? Done thinking that the world is against you?

"The world *isn't* against you, Eddie," he continued. "*You* are against you. You have to realize that no one is meant to carry the load alone. We're all in this together. Once you realize that you can ask for help, your whole world will change."

The stinging in my cheek made it hard to focus on what he was saying. "I think my world has already changed enough," I replied.

"Look, Eddie, I know life hurts terribly right now. Your grandmother and I pray every night that God will ease your pain and ours. But you are not the first young man to lose his mother, and I'm not the first man to lose his daughter. We could learn together how to miss her. You don't have to do it alone." I noticed his eyes for the first time in a long time: The piercing, look-right-through-you blue had turned tired and gray.

"I'm sorry I slapped you just now, Eddie, but I don't know who you are anymore. You are not the young man you are meant to be, and I don't know who you are allowing yourself to become. I know it's tough, but you've got to find your way through this. The hurt will pass, and, with time, you and I can learn to laugh together again." He paused and looked away. "I want my daughter back. And Eddie, I want my best friend back. I want *you* back. Sometimes I think I lost both of you in that damned car."

131

Damn was a big swear word for my grandfather. I had seen worse words appear on his face, but Grandma didn't put up with any cursing. I looked for anger, but his expression now showed only sadness and exhaustion. He looked *old.*

It occurred to me for the first time, I think, that Grandpa had lost a daughter. He needed me just as much as I needed him. Like the time on the roller coaster, we needed to squeeze each other's hands. It didn't matter who was comforting whom.

I was suddenly tired too. More than just physically; I was tired of being alone, tired of being mad all the time, tired of keeping my guilt caged in the pit of my stomach. I wanted to fall into my grandfather's long arms and let him hold me and tell me everything was going to be all right. But I was still only twelve. I didn't know how to go back. I didn't know how to correct all of the mistakes I had made. I found strength in anger. I hated the words that came out next, but I couldn't stop them:

"I don't need your help, and I certainly don't need God's." My voice was calm, and I could feel the curl of the sneer on my lips.

"I know you want to be mad at someone," Grandpa replied calmly. "If you need that to get through the day, then be mad at me. But don't be angry at God. He hasn't done this to you. Things just happen. Sometimes it's a consequence of our own actions, other times it's not. Occasionally it's just that bad things happen to good people. But God's only plan is for you to be happy."

I stared at the ground, hoping he would just stop talking. He didn't. "We all face challenges and tests, some bigger than others. They're meant to strengthen us and prepare us for the road ahead. Not just for our sake, but for all those we encounter along the way. I don't know what He has planned for us, but I do know that we're meant to conquer it, Eddie. He will never leave us in a place without the strength and knowledge we need." I wondered if Grandpa had learned all of that during one of his marathon church sessions.

"His help?" I looked up and met Grandpa's steely gaze. I felt my entire body begin to heat up. "I think He's helped us enough already, don't you? If killing innocent people is some sort of challenge or test, then God is sick and His lessons are as helpful as this stupid chicken coop. Which, by the way, I haven't finished yet." I bent down and picked up another old barn board. As I walked away I muttered something just loud enough for Grandpa to hear. "I'll let you know when I'm done."

On the last day of school one of my teachers stopped me in the hallway and put her hand on my shoulder. "Eddie, have you met Taylor?"

"I don't think so," I answered, wondering why she cared. She produced a boy my age from somewhere behind her.

"Taylor, this is Eddie. Eddie, Taylor." She stood in front of and between us, a hand on each of our shoulders. "You two are neighbors. Did you know that?"

"I haven't seen you before," I said to the gangly boy. His chocolate brown hair was curly and shot out in every direction. It was obvious that no amount of spit could tame it.

"I don't ride the bus," he answered.

We stood there looking awkwardly at each other. The teacher—her good deed now done—smiled and walked away.

"Where do you live?" I asked.

"Out on Route 161 a ways."

"Me, too."

134

"You want a ride home? The bus stinks."

I didn't know if he meant it figuratively or literally. Either way, he was right.

We walked out a side entrance and up to a long tan car. "Wow," I asked, "is this yours?"

Taylor seemed to like the fact that I thought it was cool. "No, we stole it," he replied. It was my first taste of Taylor's never-ending sarcasm.

The car was a brand-new, mammoth Lincoln Continental Mark V, and while it was unlike anything I'd ever been in before, it really wasn't "cool" so much as it was impressive to a kid who was used to bread-bag shoes. "Is your dad a doctor or something?" I asked.

"Actually, yeah," Taylor replied. "He's a brain surgeon."

"Really?" Coming from a family of bakers, that was even more impressive than the car.

"No, gotcha again. Boy, Eddie, you're really easy to fool. My dad is actually a salesman." Taylor smiled and opened the door. His parents were in the front seat.

"Who's your friend?" Taylor's mother asked.

135

"This is Eddie."

"Hello, Eddie. I'm Janice, Taylor's mother, and this is Stan, his dad."

"Hi, Eddie," Stan said.

"Nice to meet you, Mr. and Mrs . . ."

"Ashton," they said in unison, "but call us Stan and Janice."

"Mr. and Mrs. Ashton, nice to meet you."

"Same here, Eddie," Mr. Ashton said. "What's the plan, Taylor?"

136

"Eddie lives near us. I told him we could give him a ride home."

"Sure, happy to," Mr. Ashton said as he wrestled the Continental into gear. "Climb in."

"Can we talk you into joining us for dinner, Eddie?" Mrs. Ashton asked as we turned onto the road leading to my grandparents' farm. "We're going out to Taylor's favorite restaurant."

Wow, I thought. Out to eat? On a Tuesday? They must be loaded. "I'd love to . . . Stan, but my grandparents are probably expecting me." I felt weird calling an adult by his first name.

"Well, just give them a call and see if it's all right."

We got to Taylor's house a few minutes later, and I immediately called my grandmother. Her happiness over my making a new friend apparently outweighed any disappointment about my not being home for dinner. After I explained who the Ashtons were and where they lived, she reluctantly agreed to let me eat with them.

Dinner was like an adventure for me. I hardly ever got to eat out, and *never* on a regular old Tuesday. On special occasions my parents used to take me out for an All American Banana Split at Farrell's ice cream parlor, but it had to be a birthday for something like that to happen. Even still, Mom always reminded me about not ordering milk—she obviously didn't care that it came from the same place as ice cream.

I didn't know what Mr. Ashton did for a living, but he must have been rich. Not only were we allowed to order milk but we could order pop too. That was a real treat, considering the fact I didn't get to drink pop at restaurants or at home. In fact, for a long time I didn't even know what pop was, other than the fact that it had lots of bubbles.

One time, about three years earlier, I'd found a bottle of lemon-lime Alka-Seltzer in our kitchen cabinet, where we stored all the medicine. I saw the fizz that it made when you dropped a tablet in water, and figured that it was "instant pop." For the next few nights I waited until my parents had gone to bed, and then I savored the taste of what I thought was an exclusive (albeit disgusting) drink. I didn't understand why people loved pop so much, but I figured it would grow on me.

138

My clandestine soda factory was put out of business a week later when my mother had heartburn, found the half-empty bottle, and confronted me. I'd told her that I was sorry for drinking all the instant pop. She probably would've been mad if she'd been able to stop laughing.

As I now savored my *real* soda pop I noticed that Mr. Ashton was wearing a suit and tie, something that I'd never seen my father or grandfather wear outside of church. I wasn't a clothing expert, but his suit looked expensive, and I could tell that Mr. Ashton's shirt wasn't exactly homemade.

I was so busy noticing all the expensive things they had that I didn't notice how little the Ashtons actually spoke to each other.

About halfway through dinner Mr. Ashton broke the silence by saying that he had a surprise. He had some work to do in Southern California, and he was going to take the family with him so they could all go to Disneyland for a week. To my surprise, Taylor didn't look the least bit excited. In fact, he looked angry. "Oh, come on," he said, "not again. I'm so sick of going there."

I couldn't believe it. How many times had they gone? What kid could ever be sick of Disneyland? "If you guys want to go," Taylor continued, "that's fine, but I'm staying home."

There were a few moments of uncomfortable silence. I was prepared for Taylor to get the "Now you listen here, young man" speech that I would've gotten had I made a comment like that, but it never came. Instead, Taylor's mom simply replied, "Oh, well, maybe that would be okay."

What? I couldn't believe this family!

"You know, Taylor," his father continued while staring down at his meal, "if that's what you want to do, then I think it's fine. The last thing I want to do is drag you around to someplace you don't want to go. Maybe we can find somewhere else to go later in the summer."

I wanted to shout out, "You can drag *me* around!" but I think I was still in shock. Not only did Taylor not want to go on vacation to California but he'd also told his parents he was going to stay home and they'd said yes! He was my new hero. It was as if Taylor had been a grown-up and his parents had treated him as such. My grandparents could sure learn a lot from Stan and Janice. They were the perfect family.

"Thank you so much for having Eddie over for dinner," my grandmother said through the rolled-down window of the Ashtons' giant Continental.

"You're welcome. It's nice to know that these two boys each have someone nearby for the summer." The two women shared a look I recognized from watching my mother and Aunt Cathryn together.

"We'll have to invite . . ." My grandmother's voice trailed off as she looked at Taylor.

"Taylor . . ."

". . . Taylor over for a visit soon."

Mrs. Ashton drove away, and my grandmother stood, smiling, between me and the house.

"What a nice turn of events, don't you think, Eddie?"

141

"I guess." I walked past her and through the front door. She didn't come in. In fact, she didn't move at all. She just stood there looking at where I had been standing.

I had never hurt my grandmother like that before, but in that moment I didn't really even notice. I was too busy thinking about how great Taylor's life was and wishing I could be part of his family. I unknowingly made a decision that would impact Taylor and me greatly: I planned to erase the past by ignoring it.

And Grandma was part of the past.

Nine

 spent a lot of time at the Ashtons' house that summer. Aside from age, Janice had nothing in common with my mother, and that was okay with me. I didn't want to be around anyone that reminded me of all that I'd done and said, or, more importantly, *not* done and said.

I didn't realize it until much later, but Mrs. Ashton was very lonely. I never saw her drunk, but she hardly ever spent an afternoon without a crystal tumbler nearby. At the time I just assumed that it was all part of the life that "rich" people lived. It seemed glamorous. I felt at home.

Mrs. Ashton's whole life revolved around Taylor. She spent nearly all of her time and attention on making him, and now "us," happy. It was a relief, a respite from what had become my daily reality. There wasn't any past with the Ashtons, only a future. And it was bright.

Their family was very different from what I was used to. What they didn't have in laughter, they more than made up for with money. Taylor didn't wear bread bags for boots (in fact he didn't wear boots at all if he didn't want to), and his parents would give him a bike any time he wanted one. I saw at least three of them sitting idly in their garage next to the Continental.

Mr. Ashton was as tall and quiet as the house became when he was in it, which wasn't all that often. His sales job required a lot of travel, but every time he came home from a trip he brought another gift with him. I thought it was great that he and Taylor never talked much. No talking meant no lectures.

One recent trip ended with Taylor getting a brand-new TV game called Pong. Another time, after he'd been gone a long time, Mr. Ashton came back with a brand-new

144

twenty-five-inch color television set. It was beautiful. Who needed to talk when everything was "in living color"?

When I was growing up, our TV was so small that I would sit on the floor right in front of it to see better. Mom always told me that I would get cancer or go blind sitting so close to the TV set, but Dad said she was just trying to scare me. In retrospect, I think he only said that because I was his personal remote control. Every once in a while he would call out, "Eddie, four. Five. Try seven."

It never seemed right that I was the one who sat close to the television and he was the one who got the cancer.

145

Taylor didn't know how great he had it. Just looking around their modern, Brady Bunch–style house, you could tell they were happy. They even had a real remote control. Taylor would probably never get cancer or go blind and not even know why.

After a while, I began to convince myself that I was a part of their family—even more than my "real" family just a few farms away. They didn't have any problems, and life there was easy; it was what a real family was supposed to be like. Mom had always told me that "stuff" couldn't make you happy, but I realized that she had been wrong. Taylor had a bunch of stuff, and he was happier than I had ever been.

What at first seemed like a long walk to Taylor's got shorter and shorter each time I made it. One of the farms along the way was overgrown and seemed abandoned, but on one of my trips home, I discovered that I was wrong.

"Afternoon," the well-worn man said as he leaned on one of the few sturdy sections of fence along the road. He was about as old as my grandfather but leaner and quite a bit shorter. His eyes looked like they belonged to a much younger man, but his face was nearly caked with dirt, and his full, speckled beard sprang from his face as if trying to escape. If I hadn't been standing outside his farm, I'd have thought he was homeless.

"Hello," I answered, stopping a few feet away from him.

"On your way from your pal's house, are ya?"

"Yes, sir," I answered, uncomfortable that he knew where I was coming from.

"I'll bet you feel at home there," he said with understanding.

"Yes, sir."

"Well, we've both got things to do and people to see. You have a nice evening."

"You, too," I answered. I took a few cautious steps, then turned to see if he was watching me.

He was.

"Sorry to hear about your mother," he said in a voice that had changed so drastically from what I'd just heard that it could have come from a different person. His eyes were fixed on mine, but his face appeared completely relaxed. "But all is well, son. All is well."

147

Those words, my grandfather's words, instantly brought me back to Mom's funeral. I couldn't move or even look away; the man's gentle face and deep blue eyes had transformed into something else. My mother's face came to me so intensely that I could no longer see the stranger—I could only see the last few days of her life running backward in front of me.

She was painted and peaceful in a cheap casket.

She was tired and hurt in the car headed home from the farm.

She was disappointed and humiliated standing over a sweater on my floor.

She was forcing down a bitter square of Baker's chocolate.

Grief exploded within me, forcing out sobs and streams of tears, which poured down my cheeks. I sank to the ground and sat in the rough grass, cross-legged, with my face in my hands. I cried for the first time since my mother died.

After my shoulders heaved for the last time, I looked through bleary eyes toward the fence and the stranger.

I couldn't believe it—he was smiling. He began walking back toward the farmhouse. Then he stopped and turned around, his eyes meeting mine. "Until we meet again, Eddie."

"Grandpa, who lives in that run-down farm next door?" I asked that night at dinner, still a little shaken from my earlier encounter.

"Nobody, Eddie. It's been vacant for six or seven years. The Johnsons still own it, but they moved back East."

"Well, somebody's over there. A man was at the fence, and he talked to me."

My grandfather stopped chasing peas around his plate and narrowed his gaze. His bushy white eyebrows almost met above his nose. "What did he say?"

I wasn't sure whether or not to answer. "He was trying to be nice, I think. He knew I was coming from Taylor's house, and he just wanted to say hello."

"What else?" Grandpa asked, noticing my hesitation.

149

"He knew about Mom and said he was real sorry but that everything would be okay."

Grandpa looked over at my grandmother and then back to me. "Everybody knows everybody's business on this road, Eddie, and I guess it's possible some neighbor was checking up on the place."

"He kind of looked like he belonged there."

Grandma tried to hide it, but I caught her flash a worried expression to Grandpa. I knew the look well, because I'd seen it about a year earlier. We were sitting around the table having dinner when the phone rang. Grandma answered and, without saying a word, gave Grandpa the same look that I'd just seen.

A neighbor who lived at the end of the street was away and someone had broken into his house. As word spread, guys from the neighborhood ran toward the home—rifles in hand. They reached the Bauer farm just in time to catch the guy as he ran out the side door. They pinned him down and held him at gunpoint—actually, at eight gunpoints—until the police arrived.

The cop could barely contain his laughter as he walked up and saw the impromptu vigilante mob that had formed. "Boy, you're either not from around here or you're the dumbest criminal I've ever met," he said to the man with his face in the dirt. "This has got to be the safest road in the county. These people would give the shirt off their backs or the bullets out of their guns for each other."

The men all silently nodded and smiled to themselves in a rare moment of recognition about how wonderful life was on their little road. The officer continued, "Normally I'm called out to protect the homeowner, but in your case,

I actually think I'm here to protect you." The men all laughed as the would-be robber was put into cuffs.

Now, as I saw the same worried glance on my grandmother's face, I knew exactly what it meant: Grandpa would be personally checking out the Johnsons' place—and he'd likely be bringing David Bauer and some of the other neighbors, along with a few Winchester lever-action rifles, with him.

I went to bed early, but I was afraid to sleep. My mother had been a character in some of my dreams before, but always in a dull, black-and-white way. I'd never had a dream so vivid as what I'd experienced on the road that day—and I didn't want them to start now.

Unlike the Ashtons, my grandparents had an old color console Zenith television set that they'd bought at an auction. About fifteen minutes before we were going to watch a show, my grandfather would say, "I'm gonna go in and warm up the set." It took forever before the picture finally came on and looked right (with "right" in this case

151

meaning colors that always made everyone look a little seasick).

The one show that my grandparents never missed was Lawrence Welk's. Grandma loved him, but now that I'd seen Taylor's TV, Lawrence Welk only annoyed me. The show was anything but "Wonderful, wonderful!" and watching him was a constant reminder that I wasn't able to see *Starsky and Hutch* or even *Happy Days*, which Grandma called a "cute" show, except for "that Fonzie Boy."

But while I hated Lawrence Welk, I loved the idea of television. It amazed me that a camera somewhere in Welkland captured him leading an orchestra and that a moving image somehow made it through the air to the big device humming in the living room. When Grandma turned the television off, I would keep watching as the picture collapsed on itself until nothing was left but a fading dot in the center of the screen.

That night, after tossing and turning in bed for an hour, I snuck down to the family room and turned the television on. The control made a thunk so loud that I was

152

sure one of my grandparents would come to see what the noise was. I didn't dare turn the channel selector; it made even more noise than the power switch.

As I waited for the picture to materialize, I noticed for the first time how old their TV set was. I wondered if it bothered my grandmother that Grandpa couldn't afford a new one. It sure bothered me.

I sat right next to the screen—way too close to avoid getting cancer or going blind. That was when the cast of characters in my new life at the farm became complete: There were my grandparents; Taylor and his folks; the stranger next door; and my three newest friends—Johnny, Ed, and Doc.

153

I watched *The Tonight Show* that night and, at least for an hour, escaped the farm and my thoughts. I would have watched all night, but the station signed off after the show ended, leaving me with an American flag waving as "The Star Spangled Banner" played in the background.

Then there was just an Indian head on top of an odd circle—and I was alone again.

Ten

hen I told Taylor that my grandparents
only watched TV once a week and when
we did it was Lawrence Welk, he was shocked. His parents let him watch whatever he wanted, as long as he finished his chores in the summer and his homework during
the school year. Every Tuesday night he taunted me by
watching *Happy Days* and *Laverne & Shirley*. His parents
even let him stay up to watch some show called *Soap*. Taylor said it was about a puppet and some guy who thought
he was invisible. Sounded pretty weird to me, but even
puppets would've been better than Lawrence Welk.

But while television was a great excuse for me to sleep over at Taylor's house, the real reason I wanted to spend more time there was that the Ashtons treated me like a son. I imagined living there, Taylor and I hanging out and doing whatever we wanted, both of us so sick of Disneyland that we actually begged his parents to take us someplace new.

"Grandma," I said as I headed for the door late on a September afternoon, a green, tattered army-surplus knapsack that Grandpa had given me slung over one shoulder, "I'm goin' over to Taylor's for the night."

"No, you're not, Eddie. You have spent three of the last seven nights there and I'm sure that you must be wearing out your welcome."

"The Ashtons don't mind. Really. Call and ask them if you want." I was trying out Taylor's tactic of just telling them how it would be.

"They are just too polite to say otherwise." Grandma wasn't caving as easily as the Ashtons did. "You need to stay here tonight. I'll make Sloppy Joes."

"I don't want Sloppy Joes. Stan and Janice were going to take Taylor and me out to eat. We had plans!"

My grandmother took a few moments to get over her shock at my casual use of the Ashtons' first names. She didn't like it. "I'm sorry that my cooking isn't up to your new five-star standards, but if you had plans, maybe you should have run them by your grandfather or me first." Grandma's voice was kind but firm.

"But Grandma"—I had one final bullet left in my chamber—"school starts next week, and after that I'll only get to sleep over there on weekends."

157

"No, Eddie. Not tonight. In fact, you won't be sleeping over there until you are settled in at school and we see how your homework is coming."

I couldn't believe it. I'd had enough. I took my knapsack by one strap and threw it. I only intended for it to go a few feet, but I'd given it a good swing. It flew through the air and crashed against the wall, leaving a big dent in the plaster.

Grandma stared at me in disbelief for a moment. "You

are very lucky that your grandfather wasn't here to see that." The kindness had disappeared from her voice.

"Yeah, I'm feeling *really* lucky lately!" The words escaped from my mouth as I stormed up to my room. My grandfather had only laid a hand on me that one time, but I couldn't even imagine how he was going to react to how I'd just treated my grandmother. I was sure he would beat me with some exotic farm implement.

Deep inside I also knew that I deserved whatever punishment I would get. That pushed me even further away.

158

About an hour later I heard Grandpa's pickup backfire as he pulled up the driveway. The noise made me remember how much I hated that old truck. A few moments later I heard the front door open and close and then my grandmother's muffled, calm voice. Grandpa's voice answered and was not nearly as calm.

"He did what?!?" he yelled. Then more muffled Grandma followed by a slightly less upset Grandpa.

I gradually relaxed.

He never came upstairs.

The next morning I showed up at breakfast expecting the worst, but nothing happened. They were both quiet and said pleasant, if somewhat reserved, "good mornings" to me.

After breakfast I walked through the living room and saw that the wall had been repaired. If it hadn't been just a bit whiter than the surrounding area, it would have been impossible to tell where I had damaged it. My grandfather must have vented his anger with plaster and a trowel. A bucket of paint was sitting on the floor in front of the wall.

159

"Eddie, it looks like you have some painting to do," Grandpa said without looking up from his paper. "Be careful not to splatter on the floor."

"Yes, sir," I said without an ounce of sarcasm. I think that might have been the only time I called my grandfather "sir" in my entire life.

I wondered if they were as miserable with me living there as I was.

I was afraid to ask to go over to Taylor's house until the knapsack incident was forgotten, so instead he came over to our farm nearly every day for the next few weeks. My grandparents treated him just like the Ashtons treated me.

It occurred to me that having Taylor over was almost as good as being at his place. Grandma was so happy to have me close by that a simple "Aww, but Grandma, we were about to go exploring" was all it took to get out of my chores. Grandpa was harder to game, but at least Taylor was willing to help do whatever my grandfather asked of us.

One day Grandpa asked us to walk the fence line around the farm looking for sections needing repair. It was a crisp, late-fall afternoon, and Taylor and I had grand plans that did not include trudging along what seemed like a thousand miles of fence.

"It's a gorgeous day," Grandpa tried to reason, "and the walk will do you two good. Who knows, it might even turn out to be fun."

Taylor always had a better outlook than I did. He accepted the challenge as an opportunity to have an adventure. After all, our task would take us to corners of the farm that even I had not yet seen. Grandma made sandwiches for us, wrapped them up in waxed paper along with garlic pickles, and put them into my knapsack. I was a little embarrassed by Grandma's homemade bread and waxed paper, since Taylor always had store-bought bread and plastic bags. I hoped he wouldn't notice how we lived. I filled my canteen with water, joking that we needed to rough it like Lewis and Clark.

Our trip took us around the back of the property and into an area where the woods were reclaiming part of the farm. The fence was doing its best to hold off the hordes of bushes and saplings, but we discovered a few places where the forest had won.

When we were safely out of earshot of my grandparents, I decided to tell Taylor how much I liked staying at his house. "Your parents are the best. Sometimes I wish I lived with you guys."

"Seriously?" Taylor seemed surprised. "To be honest, I'd rather live with you. Your grandma is the best cook ever, and your grandpa is hilarious. The other day when I was waiting for you to finish your chores out back, he and I had a lot of fun playing cards together. It was weird, though, cause your grandma kept shouting his name from the kitchen."

I was shocked. I hadn't played cards with Grandpa since before last Christmas. I didn't want Taylor playing with him if I couldn't. "Taylor, he cheats," I sneered.

"Oh, I know," Taylor replied matter-of-factly, as if I'd been the gullible one. "That's what makes it to so great. He's been working on a system for a while now. He said that if we play just a few more times, he'll have it down and then he'll teach it to me."

162

The thought of Taylor playing cards with my grandfather really infuriated me. I wasn't mad at Taylor, I was mad at Grandpa. Taylor was *my* friend, and I didn't like Grandpa talking to him. I tried a new tactic. "Yeah," I said, "he seems pretty funny at first, but once you get to know him he's not all that great. The jokes really get old after a while. But your family is *always* great. Your parents let you do whatever you want. You guys go on great vacations. You can watch any TV show you want, and your dad told me that you guys are getting a Betamax soon so you can record shows and watch 'em over and over. What's wrong with you, Taylor? Your dad isn't a failure. You guys are rich. You have it made."

"Things aren't always like they seem, Eddie," Taylor muttered, almost as if he'd been talking to himself. He shrugged and walked a few steps in front of me, a clear sign that he didn't really want to talk about it anymore.

A tree had fallen across the fence in a corner of the wooded area, creating a notable breach and a place to sit and eat our lunch. It was also the only place where we could be inside the fence and not see any other evidence that we were on the farm. I don't know if my grandfather had planned it that way, but the trek was turning out to be one of our best adventures ever.

"Uh-oh," Taylor said to the pickle he didn't want to eat.

"What?"

"My dad's going to kill me. I was supposed to be home by three, and it's way past that."

"Just tell him you forgot. That's mostly the truth, isn't

163

it? Finish the walk with me, stay for dinner, and then walk in your house like nothing's wrong. Come on, I already know Grandpa's system. You don't need to play cards with him, I'll teach it to you," I lied.

"I can't. We're going to my aunt's house for some big family thing. I don't even know what it is, but my parents have been making a huge deal over it. Seriously, if I miss it, they'll kill me."

I pictured Taylor blindfolded against the wall as his parents stood in front of him with old-fashioned rifles. "Any final requests?" I joked, pointing a pickle at him like a gun.

"You are so weird. Things that are serious aren't, and things that shouldn't be are."

"Huh? What the heck are you talking about?"

"Never mind, Eddie. Your grandpa said that if we finished the fence today we could go on some errand with him tomorrow, so just tell him we finished." He stood up, brushed the crumbs from his pants, and started along the only section of fence we had yet to examine.

I ran to catch up with him, and we both jogged toward

the front of the farm, half looking at the fence. We could have overlooked openings big enough for an elephant to walk through, but I guess I had a lot of experience at missing what was right in front of me.

The front edge of the fence was made of new chain link attached to sturdy metal poles. Rather then walk back to the driveway, Taylor climbed up and over the fence at the corner. "See ya," he said without looking back. He really *was* scared. I watched him run along the road, then noticed something going on next door.

165

There was a corral between the old house and the run-down barn on the farm next door. The corral couldn't be seen from the road. In fact, the fields around it were so overgrown that it was only visible through the gap in the scrubby, unharvested crops in front of me. I scaled the fence not far from where Taylor had gone over and made my way close enough to see what was going on. I was pretty sure I could stay hidden in the field for as long as I cared to watch.

The old man I'd seen before was standing in the center of the corral with his back to a very unhappy horse. His grease-stained overalls were only slightly cleaner than his face. "Shhh, sweetie, it's all right. Come and get this apple." His arm was extended, and he held a quarter of an apple in his upturned palm. "Come on, come on, come on," he said, a little quieter each time. The mare snorted and tossed her head as she moved cautiously toward the stranger. She pulled her lips from her teeth and gently but quickly took the apple from his hand. Without turning around, he slowly reached into the pocket of his dirty plaid work jacket and pulled out another piece. "Would you like another one, sweetheart?" he asked in a voice that reminded me of my last encounter with him. She took it; this time, she didn't step back before eating it.

As he turned around to face her, he looked into the field directly at me, his eyes stopping just long enough to tell me he knew I was there. He took another piece of apple out of his pocket as he looked intently at the horse's face. With one cupped hand, he put the apple under her nose and gently stroked her head with his other hand.

"We're friends now, aren't we, darlin', there's nothing to be afraid of. No one is going to hurt you."

The horse actually nodded her head, as if to agree.

"Eddie," he said without turning around. "Come out and say hello to my new friend."

I took a few steps out of the field, then turned around to look at where I had been crouched in the shadows. It was hard to imagine how he had seen me in there. I climbed the four rails that made up the side of the corral and sat on the top one. The man walked over and stood in front of me. "I don't think we've been formally introduced," he said. "My name is Russell."

167

I was again struck by how dirty he looked. His beard was not really gray, as it appeared from a distance. Instead it seemed to be naturally white, but covered with layers of dirty brown and yellow. If a living human could be described as sepia, it was Russell. He smiled, removed his cowboy hat, wiped the grimy sweat from his brow with an already filthy handkerchief, and gave me a long look.

"Russell what?" I was sure my grandparents would want to know his last name.

"Just Russell."

"Oh." I paused for a few moments and turned toward the mare. "I didn't think it was that easy to break a horse." I had never been this close to a horse that wasn't moving up and down on a pole and going around in circles.

Russell smiled. "I'm actually the third man to try and help this mare. Somehow I always seem to find myself with the horses that everyone else has given up on."

As a stranger who spoke cryptically about horses, Russell probably should have made me more leery than I was. It's hard to explain, but he gave off a warmth that made me feel comfortable and secure. He had all the dirt of every farm on earth on him—yet he felt clean, peaceful. Talking to Russell felt like talking to someone I had known my whole life.

"So you just gave her an apple?" I asked.

"No, Eddie. I just showed her that I love her. Horses have to be reminded of that sometimes. This old girl had been through some tough stuff, and then everyone gave up on her. She'd been beaten and felt abandoned. I'm just trying to help her see that she's wrong."

"How do you do that?"

"Well, it may sound funny, but I just try to remind her of who she is. These horses are trained day after day to forget the instincts and emotions they're born with. Everyone wants to feel loved, but when all you feel is alone it's tough to accomplish anything else."

He was losing me. "A horse can feel lonely?"

"Of course they can. In fact, horses are more like us than you think. They're born knowing what they're supposed to become, but they don't know who they are or how to get there. I bet it's the same with you, Eddie. People probably ask you all the time what you want to be when you grow up, but that's the wrong question, isn't it? That is like saying this horse is a workhorse, instead of saying what she really is: good, gentle, and faithful. See the difference? The 'what' doesn't matter. The question people should really ask is, *Who* do you want to be when you grow up?"

I still didn't really get it. "*Who* do I want to be? You mean like Joe Namath or Evel Knievel?"

"No, not exactly." Russell smiled. His voice didn't show

169

a hint of irritation that I didn't understand what he was trying to say. "I mean who do *you* want to be? What kind of person do you want to become?"

"I want to be rich and live far away from here. I am going to have a huge house somewhere like New York City. I'll buy the fanciest car, a new TV, and anything else I want."

"Wow," Russell said, turning to face the horse. "Sounds like you've got it all figured out."

"I do. I just have to get away from here and all the people who are trying to drag me down."

Russell paused for a moment and stroked the mare's head. "So if you've got all that figured out, then you must know *who* you are."

"I already told you, I'm Eddie." I made up for Russell's patience with a severe lack of my own.

"No, I don't mean it like that. I'm sure you already know this, Eddie," Russell played to my ego, "but most people aren't like you. Most people don't know what they are going to do or where they are going to live or even what tomorrow holds. They just keep moving, hoping that the next move or the next job or the next day they'll just 'be happy.' But a guy like you gets it. That's why you've been able to make such a great plan."

I didn't quite understand why I was getting so many compliments. But I liked them. "You bet. I have it all mapped out."

"Good for you. You know people are meant to be happy, Eddie, but sometimes that's hard to do if you've allowed yourself to become someone you're not."

Now I was starting to understand what he was talking about. "Yeah, my grandfather is like that. He's so busy convincing himself that he's happy that he doesn't even notice how many things he doesn't have."

"Really?" Russell said. He seemed genuinely interested.

"Yep. I used to think he was cool and fun, but now I know exactly who he is: an old man who's fooled himself into thinking that he's successful. He can't even see that you'll never find happiness on a street full of farmers and simpleminded people. He can have so much more than a

171

stupid little berry farm. There is a whole world out there, but he's trapped here with a bunch of dead enders, bad memories, and outdated ways."

I could tell by the way Russell was listening that he knew exactly what I was talking about. I felt smart showing him how much I knew and sharing things that my grandparents could never understand. I was surprised that someone who looked like Russell "got it"—but he did.

"Boy, I'm sorry to hear that about your grandparents," Russell replied sympathetically. "It's too bad they can't learn a little from someone like you, someone who knows what he wants and goes out and gets it. And you know you'll succeed because you understand that the 'who' will always lead you to happiness. After that, the 'what' and the 'where' just fall into place. If your grandparents could figure that out, they might be as happy as you are. Maybe they'd even be as successful as you'll be."

Russell paused a moment and turned to the horse. "Of course, this old girl will figure all that out just as soon as I remind her that she's loved."

I ignored the horse. "I'm plenty happy," I protested, feeling compelled to reinforce an already stated fact. "And my grandparents tell me all the time that they love me."

"I'm sure. I didn't know we were talking about you."

"We aren't. I was just saying."

"Oh. Sure. You know, Eddie, you seem like a smart kid, so let me ask your advice on something."

"Okay." I played it cool, but I was happy that Russell already thought that much of me.

"Well, I've come a long way with this horse, but I still can't get her to trust me completely." He pulled another slice of apple out from his pocket and brought it up to the mare's nose. Her head flinched back violently. Russell held the apple slice steady, and the horse cautiously brought her head forward and took the apple in her mouth.

173

"I told you that she's been through some tough stuff," Russell said, "but it actually goes much deeper than that.

"When she was born her owners raised her on a farm with a bunch of other horses. Then the farm got sold and the new owners were hardly ever around." Russell turned back around to face me. He was almost as good a story-teller as Grandpa. "They hired someone to care for the animals, but he was a mean old guy who was more interested in abusing the horses than feeding or grooming them."

I pictured the gentle horse that stood in front of me being mistreated. It made me angry. I wanted to help her.

"Anyway," Russell continued, "one day an older horse on the farm got sick. Instead of nursing it back to health, the caretaker grabbed his rifle and killed it—right in front of this poor girl. Imagine that, seeing your friend killed for no reason, right in front of your eyes."

174

Flashes of bright lights and loud sirens filled my head. My father, frail and sick in a hospital bed. Mom, tired and angry, behind the wheel of our car.

"A few months later, a bad storm blew down a part of the fence around the corral. The horses' instincts took over, and they all ran for freedom through the breach in the fence. That's when I found her, scared and alone in the woods."

I looked back at the mare with a new level of appreciation.

"I wanted to see about buying her, so I went over to see the caretaker. He made me an offer I couldn't refuse, and I've been nursing her back to health ever since."

Russell turned back toward her and pulled out another piece of apple. "Unfortunately, she had such a bad experience that she's never trusted another human." The mare's head flinched again. "I show her love every day, but I think, in her mind at least, she equates it with fear. So, Eddie, I guess I could use your advice . . . how do I get her to realize that not everyone wants to hurt her?"

I'd gotten so engrossed in the story that I'd forgotten Russell was looking for my help. I tried to think of something smart to say. "Well, I don't know. I guess you just have to stick with what you're doing. I'm sure she'll eventually see that what happened to her wasn't her fault and that you're her friend."

I was embarrassed that I didn't have more to offer, but Russell apparently thought my answer was better than I

175

did. His face brightened. "You know, Eddie, you're absolutely right. I've just got to keep at it. Thanks."

I was glowing inside, but I didn't want to press my luck. "Well, my grandparents are expecting me," I said as I jumped down from the fence and walked away quickly.

"Come by again, Eddie," Russell offered.

I didn't have to say that I would.

That night I snuck downstairs again to watch Johnny Carson. As I came around the corner into the living room, I saw that it was lit with the flickering greenish tint of the television. My grandfather sat on the coffee table, his nose nearly touching the screen. "Grandpa?"

"Shhh," he said with a finger to his lips. Then he slid over on the table, leaving just enough room for me.

I sat next to him and we watched together in silence, wanting to laugh, but afraid to be discovered by Grandma. I could feel the hardness of his strong arm against my skinny one. For one showing of *El Dorado*, the warm feelings that we had last shared too long ago were back.

Grandpa didn't know it, but even though I was looking at the TV I was really watching the story of the last year replay in my head.

I wanted to go back but didn't know how. So instead I just sat there.

Eleven

 need your help today," Grandpa said cheerfully over breakfast the next morning. After we ate and cleared our dishes, he led me to the smaller of the two barns. The left half had been cleaned up and turned into storage for Grandma's craft supplies. She was always knitting or quilting or sewing. What was now my room had once been Grandma's old sewing room; when I'd moved in, Grandpa had moved all her stuff out here into his workshop.

The right half of the barn was still Grandpa's. The border between neatness and clutter separated the two areas just as well as any wall would have. He took me to the far corner of the barn and pulled an old sheet off what looked to me like a pile of scrap lumber.

"What are we doing, Grandpa?"

"Building your grandmother's Christmas gift," he answered. "Of course it's a *secret*," he added in a tone of mock warning.

I had completely forgotten; Christmas was just over a month away. I couldn't believe it had snuck up on me like that, probably because it had been such an unseasonably warm winter so far. Growing up, I'd always been jealous of Grandma and Grandpa, because they'd always gotten so much more snow than we had. Even though they didn't live that far away, the rain/snow line on the weatherman's map always seemed to run right between us. There had been plenty of storms where we'd been flooded and they'd had snowdrifts up to the top of their porch.

There had been times when I'd imagined myself running away and moving in with them just to get more snow days off from school. I'd pictured Grandpa and me getting up early, making a snow fort in the front yard, and drinking hot chocolate all day. Grandpa probably wouldn't even make me wear the bread-bag boots, I'd thought. It had seemed like a dream.

But now that I was living that "dream," I realized just how wrong I'd been. Sure, there were no bread-bag boots, but there was also no snow. Not one inch. There hadn't been all year. *Things aren't always what they seem.* Taylor's voice played in my mind.

Grandpa handed me some sandpaper and pointed to a stack of carefully cut pieces of wood that were arranged on the floor and on his worktable. "These need to be as smooth as a rock from the stream. Start with the coarse paper and work your way down to the fine, black paper. I've got a few more pieces to cut."

This was the last thing I felt like doing. "What are we making?" I asked, hoping I would be able to figure out a shortcut that didn't involve sandpaper.

"I think it would be more fun if I don't tell you," Grandpa replied. "Maybe you can guess as we start to put it together." He was being coy, probably because he knew why I was asking.

181

"Why don't you just go out and buy her something instead?" I suggested. "I'm sure she'd rather have something new from a store."

My grandfather looked at me like he had never seen me before. "No, she wouldn't. Besides, it makes you happier when you focus on making other people happy." They were my mother's words in my grandfather's voice.

He left me sitting alone on a stool. I sanded for a while but stopped when my hands began to cramp. It was obvious that I would never be a craftsman. The regular sounds coming from the other corner of the barn told me that Grandpa was busy and not coming to check on me anytime soon, so I began to explore. Taylor and I had snuck in a couple of times before, but I'd always been afraid that my grandfather would somehow know we'd been in there. It was the only place on the entire farm that I was forbidden to go.

I crossed over to the tidy side and began to look through my grandmother's things. There were flowers drying on a potting bench and what looked like a sewing-machine museum along the wall. There was an old Singer

182

powered only by a foot pedal connected by a leather belt to a big metal wheel. I was so intrigued by how it worked that I didn't notice the workshop had fallen silent.

Next to the old sewing machines was a set of shelves that my grandfather had obviously made by hand. They were packed with extra fabric and half-finished quilts, bolts of pajama and shirt fabric, yarn and knitting supplies. One particular ball of yarn caught my attention, and I picked it up. As I ran a strand of it between my fingers—it was rough and soft at the same time—my grandfather came and stood next to me.

183

"Some of this was your mother's. She was knitting by the time she was eight. She looked so funny; the needles were almost as long as her arms."

As he talked, I remembered Mom knitting my Christmas sweater every night, right there in front of me. I looked up at him with dry eyes. "I'm not very good at sanding."

"That's okay, Eddie. There are some things I'm not very good at either. For instance, I'm pretty rusty at raising kids. Your grandmother did most of the work with your mom. When you came along, I thought that having a grandson was going to be fun and easy. I was right . . . at least for a while."

Memories of fishing trips and ice cream cones and rigged card games flashed through my mind. It had been so long since we'd done any of the fun things we used to.

Things were different now.

Grandpa paused, as if he was trying to collect himself. When he spoke again, his voice was lower and unsteady. "Son, you and I are very much the same. We're stubborn. We always want to show people how wrong they are, how we don't need anyone but ourselves. Well, I want you to know how wrong I was. I was trying to teach you a lesson, and instead I missed what was right in front of me: your mom was too tired to drive that night. I made a mistake, and I'll regret it until the day that I die."

I wanted to drop the yarn in my hands and wrap my arms around Grandpa. I wanted so badly for things to be the way they were before. I thought about what Russell had told me. Did Grandpa really even know *who* he was? Was he really happy? Could he be feeling as lonely and abandoned as I was?

Before I could say anything, Grandpa went on. "Sometimes our strengths are also our weaknesses. Sometimes to be strong you have to first be weak. You have to share your burdens; you have to lean on other people while you face your problems and yourself. That's hard to do, but your family is there to provide a shelter from the storms that come in everyone's life."

The yarn suddenly felt alive in my hands. I imagined Mom finishing my sweater, cutting the last bit off with her teeth. She must have been so proud. Then I saw my mother staring at that sweater rolled up in a ball on my bedroom floor. The thought of it brought back a rash of emotions, none of them good. I focused on my grandfather.

Then, once again, I pushed him away.

"I don't want any help," I spat. "Everyone I've ever loved has been taken from me. I'm not letting that happen again. I don't need *anyone*. I know who I am. I'm not like you and I never will be. I'm going to be rich. I won't have to be cheap with the woman I claim to love and *make* her a present—I'll buy her a real one. My kids will have what they need."

185

I threw the yarn down as if it had been a snake and turned to run. My grandfather stepped in front of me and clamped his hands onto my shoulders. I knew that struggling wouldn't do me any good, so I just struck as defiant a pose as I could and stared straight ahead into his chest.

"Look at me." I didn't move my head; I just rolled my eyes up until I was looking into his. "First of all, I love you, Eddie, and I'm not going anywhere. Neither is your grandmother."

"You can't promise that," I protested. I couldn't let him in. "You don't know." I didn't even hear the first part of what he'd said.

"You're right, I *don't* know, but you can't live the rest of your life in fear, guilt, and anger forever. Like it or not, life is a series of events that we don't always understand or appreciate. What happened to your mother isn't your fault and it isn't mine. It was an accident. Just a stupid accident."

I was right on the verge of a complete breakdown. All of the hurt, all of the pain, all of the memories wanted to burst through at once. "Eddie," Grandpa continued, "I think you have a basic misunderstanding of what you *want* and what you *need*. We don't always get what we want, but the things that you've wanted lately, you certainly don't need."

My swirling emotions turned directly into anger. I said the most hurtful thing I could think of. "So I guess I didn't *need* a mom or a dad then."

I was trying to trap him, hoping he would lash out at me. It would have been easier for us both if we'd just stopped talking, but Grandpa wasn't going to be played that easily. "Eddie, we can't control what happens to us, but we can control how we react to it. We are all *meant* to be happy. Even you, Eddie, as hard as it is for you to believe sometimes, you are meant to be happy. If you're not happy, it's not God's fault, it's not my fault, or anyone else's fault. It's your own."

The words lit a fire inside me. I rushed to put it out before it began to melt the coldness I had come to depend on when I felt threatened by kindness. "You're only trying to make excuses for God and for yourself. I'm not happy because of *me*? Really? Where was God when Mom couldn't even keep food in the house? Where were *you* when Mom was spending every free minute turning that yarn into the only gift she could afford? I thought family was supposed to take care of family."

"You're out of line, son." He let go of me like I had let go of the yarn.

"No, I'm not. I'm right. You know it." I sensed something building inside Grandpa that I hadn't expected. Fear? Guilt? I didn't know, but I wasn't about to back down.

188

He took a step back and put a hand on a shelf full of yarn to steady himself. He considered me for a few seconds. I could tell that he was making an important decision.

"Everyone was trying to help you two, Eddie. But your mom always refused it. We aren't rich, mind you, but we could have done more than she let us. She wanted to take care of you herself—she felt like a hand-up was the same as a hand-out, and she didn't want that. She didn't want to feel like she'd failed. She was wrong, and she was stubborn. I guess you two have even more in common than I thought."

Even though I had spent my childhood wearing bread-bag boots to school, I'd never really had any idea just how much my parents had struggled. It wasn't until after my mother died that I began to piece it all together.

"Let me show you something." Grandpa squeezed between the sewing machines and the shelving and into the corner of Grandma's part of the barn. I followed him, and we stood next to each other in front of a green canvas tarp. It smelled like camping. He looked at me again as if he still wasn't sure whether he should do what he was about to. After what seemed like an eternity, he finally said, "Your mother didn't know about this. She wouldn't have liked it. She would have thought it was too much."

He grabbed the center of the tarp and pulled it away. *A brand-new Huffy.*

I was speechless. It was the gift I'd wished for but never gotten: bright red with a black vinyl banana seat and big, curved chrome handlebars.

My gaze shifted down to the tires. Twenty playing cards had been placed into the spokes of each wheel to make a custom "clicking" sound as the wheels turned. I recognized the cards immediately as being from Grandpa's favorite deck.

No wonder he wouldn't play with me that day, I thought.

My guilt multiplied. I couldn't move. My mind was a tangled mess of thoughts, memories, and emotions.

Grandpa finally broke the silence. "See, Eddie, sometimes the gift you want most is right in front of you, but you have to get out of your own way to receive it."

I couldn't speak, but the expression on my face said more than I ever could.

190

Grandpa continued, "Grandma knew that I'd taught you some of my present-hunting tricks, so she wouldn't let me hide this anywhere in the house. We planned to give it to you as soon as we were done with the other gifts, but then you gave your mother a hard time about staying over. I . . . well, I wanted to teach you a lesson." Grandpa's words trailed off as tears escaped from his eyes and slowly rolled down his cheeks.

Grandpa was crying.

"Son, if I thought something as simple as a bike could

make you happy, I would have given this to you a long time ago. But a bike can't. No material thing can. You have to find your way back to the things that will give you lasting happiness, and you can't buy them in a store."

I heard Grandpa speaking, but I was transfixed on the Huffy. I couldn't take my eyes off of it. I felt like it might disappear, just like everything else that was good in my life.

"See, Eddie, you're not alone. You never were. We didn't abandon you, or your mother, and we never will."

I felt like speaking, but I couldn't move my mouth. Everything I had made myself believe was turning out to be wrong—and I wasn't prepared to face that.

Grandpa went on, "I have some 'if onlys' about that day, too. If only I hadn't taught you how to hunt for presents. If only I hadn't tried to teach you a lesson. If only I'd demanded that you stay. If only I had given you the bike. If only I hadn't been so . . . stubborn."

I slowly shifted my gaze from the bicycle to my grandfather. His eyes were red, wet, and very tired. I considered

191

him and felt the now familiar crush of emotions weighing on me, begging me to cave in and fall into his strong arms. I pushed back with every ounce of energy I had left.

Every time I trusted someone, I got hurt. Every time I let go, I was let down. *Not again.* I would drive them away before they left.

I steadied myself and looked deep into my grandfather's eyes. "You gave me that big speech about God and happiness before, but look at you; you're not happy. You've been fooling everyone for the last year, but not me. I see right through you." I wasn't about to let go of my guilt and anger so easily, and I certainly wasn't about to share it with the person I had convinced myself was causing most of it.

Grandpa looked stunned. I went for the knockout punch. "Mom would be alive if it wasn't for *you* making us leave that day."

Now it was Grandpa's turn to be speechless. I sensed his vulnerability, and it made me even stronger. "You can go to church all you want, but none of the people there are really happy, so stop your preaching. Stop telling me how great things are because 'Jesus loves me,' and how happy we are because 'God is with us' and how 'we're the perfect little family.' It's all a lie." I was virtually shouting now. "Do you know why it's a lie? Because there is no God. Jesus doesn't love you. *Jesus doesn't care.*"

My words hung in the air, as if caught in the dusty rafters of the old barn. Tears once again began to run down my grandfather's cheeks. I went in for the kill. "I'm the only *real* one in this family. I know who I am. I will be happy when I'm far away from here, when I don't have to worry about other people doing stupid things, like making their tired daughter drive."

193

I ran from the barn with unseen tears running down my cheeks. My grandfather was left alone with a bicycle and the yarn of a hundred unmade sweaters.

I stared at my bedroom ceiling, its smooth white plaster standing in stark contrast to the cracked, water-stained ceiling of my bedroom at home. Home, where I belonged. I felt like I should be crying, but I couldn't. I wasn't sad.

I thought about the bike and all that it symbolized:

hope and happiness; death and despair. Grandpa's words flashed through my head. *You have to share your burdens; you have to lean on other people . . . We are all meant to be happy.*

They were nice sentiments, but they were just words and I was done talking; my snowball had grown too large. Russell was right—figuring out the *who* would lead to the "what" and the "where," and now I had all three answers: My grandparents' farm was the "what" and it was part of "who" I *used* to be. Now it would soon be time to show everyone the "where."

194

I got up from my bed and went over to the dresser. It had five drawers, only four of which I ever used. My sweater was in the fifth drawer, at the very bottom. It was the only thing in there.

A mirror hung on the wall just over the dresser, but I avoided looking myself in the eyes. Something inside was telling me that I was going down the wrong road and that I needed to start over with my grandparents—but I ignored it. It was easy to fool other people, but, for some reason, the mirror made it harder and harder to fool myself.

I took the sweater out, held it to my nose, and took a deep breath of my mother. I felt completely, utterly lost. My old life and the old me were gone, and she was gone with it. I was filled with regret.

I never even had a chance to say good-bye.

Twelve

 y grandfather wasted no time in picking up right where we had left off in the barn. After breakfast the next morning he followed me into the living room as Grandma cleared the dishes. "Who do you think you're hurting?" he asked with a carefully controlled voice. Yesterday's old, tired eyes were now steely blue.

"I'm just trying to get out of here."

"Well, that's not going to happen. You're going to be here for a good while. I told you yesterday, I'm not going anywhere, and, son, neither are you. In the meantime, you and I need to come to an understanding. This is not negotiable: You will obey me and respect your grandmother. She is the kindest, gentlest, most giving person you will ever meet. She has suffered enough. I can handle all of your selfish hatred, but I swear, if you break that woman's heart anymore, you're gonna have to answer to me."

I looked into the kitchen. Grandma's back was to us as she worked over the sink. For an instant I felt guilty for adding to her burden. It passed quickly.

"Just stay out of my way and I'll stay out of yours," I snorted.

198

"That's not going to work, Eddie. I'm going to love you no matter how much you fight me. I wish it wasn't that way. I'd much rather laugh and go get ice cream at the hardware store again. I want Grandma to ask us where we've been for the last three hours. I want to show you the rest of the Christmas hiding spots I've found over the years, but most of all, I just want my best friend back again."

I couldn't believe it—another lecture. And he wasn't done. "If you want to keep going down this self-pity path, that's your choice, but it's the wrong one. Either way, I'm not moving on. I'll always be here with open arms, ready to show you how good life can be if you just let someone else into it. But until then I'll be watching you like a hawk. You don't fool me, Eddie. I understand you better than you understand yourself."

"Watch me all you want. I don't care. Maybe you'll learn something. Besides, there's only one person around here who even comes *close* to understanding me—and it isn't you."

Grandpa looked confused for a second, then glanced into the kitchen.

199

"It's not Grandma," I answered with more contempt than I felt. "I'm talking about Russell!"

"Who?"

"Russell. The man who lives next door."

"Eddie, I don't know what you think you're doing, but you can stop with this Russell nonsense. I went over there with some of the neighbors a few times and we didn't see anyone, nor any sign that the Johnsons ever sold the place."

"Well then you obviously don't all know each other as

well as you thought. Russell lives there, and he *gets* it. He knows who I am."

Grandpa glared at me. "I don't even know who you are anymore, Eddie. I don't know if you really saw someone or if you're making all of this up as part of some sort of escape plot you've hatched. If that's the case, it's not going to work. Either way, just stay away from the Johnson farm. You have no business going over there without me."

"Fine," I replied, though I knew it was anything but. In that instant I realized how far my relationship with my grandfather had deteriorated. He couldn't even trust his own grandson anymore.

In what had become my normal routine, I did exactly the opposite of what my grandfather told me to.

I walked to the Johnsons' farm, through the scrub and past the corral. The mare was outside. She watched me go by and greeted me with a snort and a flick of her tail. The same horse that had been so ornery before was now so gentle. It was like a completely different horse.

The bottom step leading to the porch was gone, and I had to half jump to reach the next step. Once on the porch, I stopped and listened to the tarnished copper wind chime hanging near the door. A gentle breeze forced it to surrender a few clicks and a couple of unimpressive tones. I wondered if I shouldn't just turn around and go home.

What home?

The torn screen door opened with a squeak as the spring stretched out for the millionth time. I hesitated, then quietly knocked on the door. Small chips of ancient paint came away with my knuckles. I reached out to try again, thinking that there was no way anyone could have heard my knock. Then a gentle voice came from behind me.

"Hello, Eddie."

I should have been startled, but I wasn't. "Hi, Russell."

"I was just going to take a break. Come and sit with me a while."

He led me through tall dead grass to a big tree with a park bench under it—a real park bench. It still had a faded advertisement for the Yellow Pages.

"Auction," he said simply, answering my question before I asked it. "This is where I come to think after more
than just my fingers have done the walking." He smiled.
"Everyone needs a place where they can go to just ponder
for a while. Silence is important; it's the only time you can
hear the whispering of truth."

I wasn't sure how to respond, so I didn't say anything.

Russell let out a deep breath. "It's funny," he continued,
his voice barely audible, "how many people just look at the
surface and never ponder the deeper meaning of things. I
guess maybe it's easier that way, because when you skim
the surface you blame your problems on the first person
you find—and that's never yourself." He paused as if to
underscore what he'd just said. "Maybe that's why people
aren't comfortable with silence. Silence makes you think,
and thinking makes you realize that not all problems are
caused by someone else."

Russell had his eyes closed. I was sure he would sit
there in silence for a month if I waited for him to speak
again. The silence was awkward and uncomfortable.

202

"Aren't you afraid your horse will run away?" I asked. "Your broken fence sure isn't going to keep her here."

Russell kept his eyes closed as he considered my question. "If you treat an animal right, they don't run away. They're not like us. They run away from people they don't trust; most times we run away from ourselves."

More silence.

"I suppose I'm just about done with this old girl," Russell continued. "I think she's pretty much remembered who she is. And she is happy. There's not much more for me to do. I'll probably give her a few more days, and then I'll be hitting the road again."

Figures, I thought to myself. Everyone else I've ever been close to has left. Why wouldn't Russell?

He lifted his head and looked deep into my eyes. It felt like he was looking through me. "What can I do for you, Eddie?"

"Nothing. I just came over to say hello." Lying was becoming second nature to me.

Russell turned his head and picked up a small stick

203

from between his feet. "You know, Eddie, sometimes we get so entangled in life that we miss the obvious. We just get so caught up in our own problems that most of the time we fail to see what's—"

I finished his sentence almost by rote. "Right under our nose?"

"Yes, we fail to see the things that are closest to us. It's like the old expression 'You can't see the forest for the trees.' You're in the forest right now, Eddie, but you're too close to the trees to realize it. Maybe you need to step back and see the bigger picture."

I nodded my head in agreement: I knew Russell would understand. He already seemed to know exactly what I planned on doing—seeing the whole picture by getting as far away from this godforsaken street as possible.

Russell continued, "See, we're all made up of two parts. There's a part that *thinks* and there's a part that *feels*. Usually, the two parts work together and everything is fine, but sometimes life hits us hard and one part overtakes the other. For example, you miss your dad terribly, right, Eddie?"

I wondered how he knew about my dad, but at that point I was more curious about where this was heading. "Sure," I answered cautiously.

"Well, you *think* about him plenty, but how often do you remember the *feelings* you had when he was around? When you *think* about him now, you picture him in a hospital bed or in a casket at his funeral. You've replaced dreams with nightmares."

It was hard to argue with that. I looked at the horse.

"You've done the same thing with your mother. You've replaced good memories of pancakes and laughter with bad memories of an argument and a car wreck. You have to stop thinking so much and instead start *feeling* again, even when," he paused, then said, "no, *especially* when it hurts."

A vision of Mom lying in her casket involuntarily popped into my head, as it had done so many times before. But now, for the first time since her death, I was able to force it out and replace it with how I felt. I felt happiness and warmth, joy and sorrow—but, most of all, I felt a longing to see her again. For the first time, I *felt* how much I missed her.

205

"Eddie, your parents did a good job trying to teach you how to live your life. They showed you that no matter what happened, all would be well in the end. But look at what you've done with those lessons; you've crumpled them up into a ball and tossed them onto the floor."

I looked away. I knew he was right.

"You're not living in the present, Eddie—you're living in the past. Life is here to be shaped and molded into what you want it to be, but you've done exactly the opposite; you've let life shape and mold you. You don't know *who* you really are because, right now, you're no one. You're empty inside."

What? I was fuming. How could Russell say that? I knew exactly who I was. I was about to remind him of that, but Russell wasn't interested in my feedback. He continued, "The two most powerful words in any language are 'I am.' Those two words contain all the creative power of the heavens themselves. It was God's answer from the Burning Bush to Moses's question 'Who shall I say sent me?'—'I am that I am.' It is the name of God."

"I don't believe in God."

Russell considered me for a second. "He's sorry to hear that. Maybe it's because you've invoked his name to create something that you're not—a reality that exists only because you have made it so."

I didn't even know what he was talking about. He must've seen the confusion in my face.

"Eddie, when was the last time you honestly thought, 'I am happy; I am strong; I am a good person; I am worthy'?" His voice was powerful, commanding.

My silence said more than I ever could.

"You've spent far too much of your time turning yourself into something you are not: a victim. No one can *make* you into a victim; only *you* can do that . . . and you have. But there's another choice you can make as well—you can choose to be a *survivor*."

A flood of memories came rushing back to me.

Dad trying to teach me how to fly a kite in the street outside our house. Every time he'd get it going, another car would come around the corner and the kite would nosedive into the asphalt.

I tried to push it away.

Dad and I playing football in the backyard. He could throw the ball so far that I'd have to run to the neighbor's yard to catch it.

"Feel, Eddie, *feel*."

Dad and I walking down the middle of the street in the snow, the streetlights making his face glow.

Suddenly I felt a pit in my stomach.

"Don't think yet, son, *feel*."

Dad's face was glowing again, but now it was under the bright white lights of his hospital room. He looked tired and frail. A flash of darkness. I was at his funeral. *By His counsels guide, uphold you; With His sheep securely fold you; God be with you 'til we meet again.*

As hard as I tried, I *couldn't* feel. I was inundated with thoughts. Wave after wave, memory after memory.

I couldn't fight it anymore—it all seemed so overwhelming. I am not.

I let go. Russell had his back to me. The horse was eating gently from his hand. "You have such a bright future," he said. "You just have to believe in it."

"I think it's time for me to go home."

Russell never turned around. "Oh, that it is, Eddie. That it is."

This time, I didn't say anything to Grandpa about Russell. It didn't matter. We stopped talking any more than we absolutely had to. He'd decided that everything I did was selfish and manipulative, and his growing distrust gave me the excuse I needed to be the bitter and disrespectful thirteen-year-old that I was beginning to believe I really was.

Rather than faking a normal, happy relationship, we set in motion a nasty cycle that was sucking every ounce of goodness right out of our home.

Grandma deserved better.

It's not that Grandpa was mean to me; he just quit trying to be nice. Maybe he was just waiting for me to grow up, or maybe he'd just had enough of it all—but, whatever the reason, Grandpa answered my constant abuse with indifference. Harsh words and restricted privileges were reserved for when I broke rules or crossed the line by taking my anger out on my grandmother.

209

Unable to get sympathy at home, I looked for it at the Ashtons' instead. "I can't stay there anymore, Taylor," I said over lunch at school one day.

"Where will you go?" he asked, just as I had hoped.

"If I could just get a break for a while, maybe things would settle down."

"Let's talk to my folks," he offered.

Finally.

Thirteen

chool let out ten days before the holiday because Christmas fell on a Sunday. Grandpa had gone on his annual three-day hunting trip a little later than normal, which gave me the perfect opportunity to finally put my plan into motion.

"Grandma, would you mind if I stayed over at Taylor's house for a few nights? His parents already said it was okay." Grandpa never would've allowed this, but Grandma was a softie. She was still under the mistaken impression that I could be "saved," and I used that against her.

To my surprise, she didn't answer right away. I started to worry that I might have miscalculated.

"Grandpa wouldn't approve, but I trust you, Eddie." She looked deep into my eyes as she said, "I know your heart. I suppose it would be okay if it's just a few nights." Whew. I quietly breathed a big sigh of relief.

I ran up to my bedroom, opened my window, and heaved the duffel bag I'd stolen from the barn up onto the windowsill. It held nearly everything I owned, along with a few things I didn't, crammed into every pocket and corner. I pushed it over the edge, hoping that it wouldn't make much noise when it hit the ground.

"Good-bye, dear," Grandma said as the Ashtons pulled up in their Continental. I was surprised that no one asked why I didn't just walk, like I had a hundred times before. While Grandma made small talk with Mrs. Ashton, Taylor opened the passenger door and helped me load in the duffel bag.

I felt like I'd finally escaped.

Mr. Ashton was away on another short business trip, so Taylor and I turned our attention to treating his mother like royalty. We made her breakfast, we took out the garbage, we even vacuumed the rugs and did the dishes without being asked.

All the while we watched her like a hawk, waiting until she was in the perfect mood. Not surprisingly, it came two days later at about four o'clock in the afternoon. Mrs. Ashton was watching television, a smile on her face and a crystal tumbler in her hand, when we made our approach.

"Mom," Taylor began, "Eddie and I want to talk to you about something."

"Of course," she replied, never taking her eyes off the television. "What is it?"

Taylor looked at me; I had the stage now. I couldn't even count how many times I had rehearsed what I was about to say. I steadied my voice. "Janice," I began, "my grandparents are miserable, and so am I."

She stopped watching the television and turned to face me. I had her attention now. "They're just too old to really understand me," I continued. "Plus, I feel bad be-

215

cause Grandma just wants peace and quiet, and I'm nothing but a burden to them."

"Oh, Eddie, I'm sure that's not true."

"It is, Janice, believe me. I've tried everything, but we just don't see eye to eye anymore. I think all three of us would be much happier if I could just come and live with you guys for a while. My grandparents would be fine with it. In fact, they might not admit it, but I think secretly they're really hoping that I would ask you." It wasn't hard to sell any of this because I truly believed it. I had closed down my emotional attachments for so long that I honestly thought my grandparents would be thrilled if I left. They could get on with their lives and I could get on with mine. Besides, I knew what I wanted to do and where I was going—and it didn't include being stuck on a farm.

Mrs. Ashton's eyes narrowed. "Well, Eddie, if your grandparents are really okay with it, then so am I. But I'll have to talk about it with Stan when he gets home tomorrow."

I nodded my head and looked over at Taylor. It took every ounce of self-control I had left not to smile.

The next day marked the third day since I'd left, and I knew that my grandfather would soon be back from his trip. When he found out that I'd been gone for so long, he'd call the Ashtons, or worse, come right to their house.

Mr. Ashton had gotten home earlier that morning, and now Taylor and I were standing in front of his parents in the living room. "Eddie," Mrs. Ashton said softly, "we understand. We're more than happy to have you here, but we're going to have to make some arrangements. You and Taylor go find something to do while Stan and I try to figure something out."

"Are you ready to have a new brother?" I said smugly to Taylor after his parents left the room.

For longer than I could remember I had been looking forward to this moment as the time I would finally be happy. So why did I feel like I had when I'd opened the sweater on Christmas morning?

We're all made up of two parts. There's a part that thinks and then there's a part that feels.

That was the problem. I *felt* great, but the thinking part of me knew that I wasn't going to get what I expected—I was going to get what I deserved.

After lunch, Mr. Ashton told us to get ready to go for a drive. "I need to go to the store for your mom, Taylor. Why don't you and Eddie come along? We'll stop for a treat."

We got into the Lincoln, pulled out onto the road, and drove past Russell's farm. As usual, it looked abandoned. It wasn't long before my grandparents' house came into view. As we approached, I slouched down in my seat and hoped they weren't looking out the window. I had a new life now.

"What are you doing?!" I yelled as Mr. Ashton turned into the driveway by my grandfather's old plow and pulled up to the house. My grandmother's silhouette appeared and became sharper as we approached.

"Eddie, Janice and I came over here last night and spent nearly two hours with your grandparents. They don't see things quite the same way you do. I know it's hard to believe, but it's best for you to be here with them right now."

For a moment I considered bracing my legs against the front seat and refusing to get out of the car. I'd been betrayed. They'd hurt me. I felt as if a knife was working in a circle around my heart, twisting inside my chest and making me want to scream for help. I couldn't believe the Ashtons and my grandparents had conspired against me. It bruised my pride to think I'd been so stupid that I hadn't even seen it coming.

219

I sat in the backseat, angry, empty, confused. My left side was warm from the heater, but the open door sent chills down my arm and leg. My side hurt. My eyes burned. I fought back tears like I'd never fought anything in my life.

Mr. Ashton stood next to me, patiently holding the front passenger seat down so I could get out.

Taylor sat next to me, looking straight down at the floor. I wondered if he had betrayed me too.

A dozen crude, hateful things passed through my mind, but I said none of them. In fact, for the next twenty-four hours, I said nothing at all.

"Eddie, please, just talk to us . . ." Grandma repeated her speech about how much they loved me and how the Ashtons loved me, too. They were hurt and disappointed, but most of all, they were confused. They couldn't understand how I could possibly think they'd be happier if I left.

My grandfather seemed a little softer than he had been before I'd left, but he didn't openly gush, like Grandma. It went unsaid at the time, but Grandpa knew exactly *who* Stan Ashton really was: the big-city guy that he would've made pay to take his wood and windows away.

"Christmas is coming," he told me later that night, clearly hoping we could put the past where it belonged. "What do you say we enjoy it and start the new year off with a fresh look at things?"

"Start fresh?" I asked incredulously. Grandpa had unwittingly bent my sadness into pent-up anger that pushed its way into my face, turning it bright red. "Start *fresh*? Are you going to bring Mom and Dad back to life? Are you going to give me a life like other kids have? Like Taylor has? You think I'm supposed to just forget everything that's happened?"

"Not forget, Eddie . . . *forgive*. You don't have to move past it, but you do have to move through it. Most of the slop you are wallowing in is of your own making."

"You keep talking to me like it's going to make a difference. I'm thirteen years old, and my life is already over."

221

My grandmother stepped between us. "Eddie, you're right. We're too old to have a teenager, but we're trying really hard. We've seen a lot and we've been through a lot. We know that things will get easier—you've just got to stick with it for a while."

I stood and pulled my fist from my jean pockets. "Right." I mustered as much pain and anger as I possibly could into my gaze. I turned to my grandfather, but my stare was no match for his. "You don't want me here, and I don't want to be here. Now, thanks to you, my only friend doesn't want me either." I spun on my heels and flew into my room, slamming the door so hard that one of Grandma's pictures fell from the wall in the hallway.

It was a picture of my mother.

Less than a minute later, my door opened again and my grandfather stood there carrying the duffel bag I'd used in my escape. I'd barely been able to drag it along the ground, yet he easily lifted it with one hand, stood it on its end, and rested his palm on it as he faced me.

"Sit down, Eddie."

222

I sat on the bed and tilted my head way back to look up at him.

"This nonsense stops tonight. I have dried more of your grandmother's tears in the last year than in all our other years together—combined. Last night she told me that she wished she had died instead of your mom. You think the world is against you. Even if it were true, it wouldn't give you an excuse to treat people the way you do. You are here because we're family. You don't use family."

"I don't *have* any family," I snapped back at him. "As far as I'm concerned, my family is dead."

If we were all God's children, then I wanted to hurt one of His, just like He had hurt me. The darkness tightened all around me.

The expression on my grandfather's face completely changed. The number of strained creases stayed the same, but they changed direction as controlled anger turned to deep pain.

"Don't say that. Don't ever say that. You are everything to us, and you were everything to your parents. Eddie, you choose your own path in life. You've had a hard road and there've been wrong turns, but you'll find your way. And we'll be there to help you at every turn."

His words were welcome, but they brought me no comfort. In that moment I realized that my stubbornness was more powerful than his kindness. This was going to be the one game that Grandpa was finally going to lose, because now I was the one with the system.

I already knew how this game was going to end.

On Friday I went through all my things, jammed as much as I could into my knapsack, and hid it in the closet. The three of us spent that evening quietly staying out of each other's way. "Tomorrow's Christmas Eve, Eddie. You must be at least a little excited," Grandma said, trying to break the ice over dinner. "The weatherman says it might even finally snow!"

Sure it will, I thought, *it never snows here anymore.*

I said nothing.

224

A few hours later, I decided to sneak downstairs to watch television. I didn't know when I would have another chance to watch Johnny Carson, and, besides, I was too worked up to sleep. As I padded silently across the floor in front of my grandparents' closed bedroom door, I heard something. It was late for them to be up. I stopped to listen. The muted sounds were like what came from the TV when I had the volume down just a little too far. But it couldn't have been a television set I was hearing; they had only one.

My grandmother was saying something in between sobs. My grandfather's voice was kind and soothing. I turned around and went back to my room.

The brass clang of the alarm clock woke me from a deep sleep. It took me a minute to remember where I was and what was going on. I wiped the sleep from my eyes and looked over at the old windup alarm clock that I'd set for three o'clock. I'd put a sock on top to muffle the sound. I pushed the lever to stop the hammer and got out of bed. While it would have been more dramatic to make a rope out of sheets and escape out the window, I no longer needed drama or a good story to tell my friends. I just needed out.

I took the sweater from the bottom drawer of my dresser and held it up under my chin. It would've been a perfect fit now. I put the sweater up against the mirror hanging on the wall, the same mirror that I'd avoided look-

225

ing into for fear of seeing what I'd become. I tucked it in over the top edge and it hung there, completely covering the glass. Now the old Eddie and my Christmas sweater could finally be together. I was happy to say good-bye to both of them, and all the misery they represented, for the very last time.

In spite of my thick winter coat I managed to awkwardly work my shoulders into the straps of the heavy knapsack. I put on my stocking cap and gloves and walked quietly down the stairs, taking just one at a time and pausing after each step to let the creak settle.

226

I reached the bottom stair, exhaled, and stepped out the front door into the world.

Fourteen

t was darker than I'd expected. The patch-
work of ice covering the dead brown grass
made the last snowfall seem like a distant memory.

229

My plan was to hitchhike into town. We weren't far
from the Boeing plant, so I knew there would be cars on
the road even at this hour. But the emerging outline of the
barn gave me a better idea. I pulled my grandfather's flashlight from my coat pocket and turned it on. The batteries
were almost dead, but there was enough light for me to
make it to the barn. Pulling the door open would have
made it drag along the ground and make a horribly loud

noise, so, with the flashlight under my chin, I lifted up on the door and carefully swung it open.

The light made everything in the barn cast long, spooky shadows. The sewing-machine museum could have been a torture chamber. I headed for the camping tarp covering the present that never was. I lifted it off and felt the cold metal of the handlebars through my knit gloves. I set the flashlight on the ground and removed all the cards from the spokes so that no one would hear me leave. I noticed my grandfather had only used hearts. My grandmother's touch, I thought. I left the hearts scattered all over the floor.

I tried to maneuver the bicycle from its tight hiding place, but the kickstand caught one of the legs of the shelving unit. Skeins and balls of yarn tumbled to the floor in slow motion. I guided the bike through the mess and out the door.

I was afraid that all of the noise might have woken my grandparents up, so I breathed a heavy sigh of relief when the house behind me remained dark as Grandpa's plow finally came into view. Still, I knew it wouldn't be long before Grandpa was up doing chores and would notice that I was gone. I doubted he cared enough to get in his truck and go looking for me, but Grandma was a different matter. If anyone would care that I was gone, it would be her. And she could be pretty persuasive when she wanted to be.

Would someone really come for me?

Mount Vernon was an hour and a half away by car. I had no idea how long it would take on a bike. I hoped I could make it there by nightfall. Fortunately, a few months earlier, Taylor had shown me a shortcut to the main highway. It ran through a nearby cornfield just past his home. Not only would it save time but it would also keep me off the main road, just in case Grandpa came looking.

Would someone really come for me?

I turned left, riding in the narrow, matted, grassy space between the white line and the drainage ditch. As my eyes adjusted to the predawn darkness, I saw the opening to Russell's overgrown driveway.

The grind of my bike's chain and tires were the only

231

sounds I heard at first. Then wind moving through barren trees joined the chorus. Then there was nothing but the sound of my own breathing.

Russell's house was completely dark. I turned my flashlight back on, then wandered off the driveway and headed toward the corral. I expected the dim yellow beam to reveal a sleepy mare. Instead it was empty.

I parked the bike next to the house and carefully navigated the porch steps. There was something wrong with the silence. I aimed the flashlight to where the wind chime should have been. Nothing. I turned the light off and looked through the window, straining to find any sign of life in the house. Nothing. I aimed the light toward the big tree where we had sat on the park bench. It was gone.

And so was Russell.

With Russell gone, there was nothing, and nobody, I would ever miss about this stupid cow town. I got back on my bike, followed the moon down the driveway to the main road, and headed toward town. For the first time in my life, I was completely and totally free. And it *felt* great.

After a few more minutes of pedaling, Taylor's driveway came into view. I was glad that I didn't have time to act on the anger churning in my stomach, since his mailbox was due for a good bashing.

Instead I just pedaled. Not saying good-bye would have to be good enough revenge. Ahead of me I saw the narrow dirt road Taylor had told me about. I steered my bike toward it. The dirt-and-gravel trail was deeply rutted and lined on both sides by a dense, gray wall of dead and decaying cornstalks. As I rode, familiar farms gave way to unfamiliar sights. The sky was clear now and the moonlight helped me dodge the deeper scars in the path. *No one will ever find me*, I thought. *No one is looking anyway.* The thought filled my heart with anger.

233

In the solitude of the cornfield I could say whatever I wanted and no one would hear me. No one but God. It was an opportunity for me to vent my rage.

"I hate you!" I shouted. The night sky seemed to swallow my words. There wasn't even an echo. I pedaled faster.

"I asked you to help my mother be happy, and you couldn't do that. Instead, you took her from me when I needed her most. My dad was a good man, and you couldn't have cared less about him." I paused, as if expecting a reply. None came. I poured all of my anger into the pedals.

I felt so alone. Screaming into the nothingness was the only thing that gave me comfort. "All I asked you for was this stupid bike, and even that was too much for you. You're nothing but a fraud! I hate you!"

At that moment, words echoed through the cornstalks and into my mind. They seemed to be coming from everywhere, and nowhere, all at once. The voice sounded a lot like my own, but my thoughts never had that much power or clarity.

"*Sometimes the gift we want most is already with us, but we have to get out of our own way to receive it.*"

I gritted my teeth and stood up on the pedals. "It's not my fault!" I screamed as loud as I could, pedaling even faster—as if trying to outrun the voice. Suddenly my front tire caught a rut, throwing the bike sideways across the path. I screamed as I hit the dirt road. I don't know how

234

long I lay there, but when I finally sat up, the moon was gone. But the voices weren't.

"*Come home, Eddie. Just come home.*"

"No!" I shouted. "I don't have a home!"

The voice echoed words I'd heard somewhere before. "*Animals run away from people they don't trust; most times we run away from ourselves.*"

For good reason, I thought. I couldn't stand to be around myself anymore. I'd turned into something I hated, and I'd blamed it on everyone and everything else.

I stood up slowly and walked over to inspect the bike. The chain was off and the front fork was completely bent, as was the tire rim, rendering both useless. Now what would I do?

"*You can't run away from yourself,*" whispered the voice.

"Wanna bet?" I shouted.

I began running, at first down the dirt path and then into the field itself, half blind from covering my eyes from the stinging, whipping cornstalks. A dozen yards ahead of me, a flock of crows flew up from the field, screeching wildly.

235

My heart was pounding so hard that I thought I could see it beating through my coat. I collapsed to my knees and looked up at the predawn sky. "I hate you," I said softly.

"*I love you,*" the voice whispered back.

I lay there for a long time, aching and exhausted. I had been running from these strange voices, but now my head was filled with my own.

Why didn't I talk to Grandpa? Why did I always pull back when he and Grandma tried to reach out? Why did I try to hurt my mother?

"*I love you,*" the voice repeated. "*Come home, Eddie. All is well.*"

How could all be well? How could anything ever be well again? At that moment I began to shed the first unselfish tears of my entire life. I had cried before, but this time it came from someplace deeper. Images of my family flashed through my mind. *I loved them. I hated myself.* Deep inside I wanted their forgiveness.

Look at yourself, I thought. I was just thirteen, and I was already as broken as the corn around me. This isn't what life was supposed to be. But when had life ever been what it was supposed to be? I wished I could start over again. I wished I had a second chance to do the right things, but I knew better: There are no second chances.

How could anyone ever forgive me after all the things I'd done? How could I look Grandpa in the eyes knowing that all he would see was the kid I had turned into over the last year? I was as empty and as dead inside as the cornfield I stood in. Maybe this was where I belonged. Maybe this was my new home.

After a few more minutes I wiped my eyes, lifted my backpack, and stumbled to my feet. I wandered back in the direction I thought I had come from, following a trail of gray, broken stalks. I had no idea where I was or how far I'd come in my mad rush into the field. I climbed a small knoll, high enough to look over the top of the corn and survey the area. I looked in the direction I'd thought I'd come from, but the road was gone and there was no sign of my bike.

Nothing looked familiar. The land was flat, dead, and barren, an endless pattern of brown, black, and gray corn-

237

stalks as far as I could see. Then, as I looked behind me, I saw a road. But it wasn't the one I had traveled earlier. It was broken and desolate, and at the end of it lurked something that filled me with terror: a dark, undulating storm.

Where had it come from? Why hadn't I seen it earlier?

A new, brash voice spoke to me. It seemed to come from the cornfield itself. *"You were right, Eddie, God doesn't care. He never has."* The words echoed my own thoughts and should've been comforting, but the tone of the voice sent a shiver down my spine.

238

The now familiar soft whisper responded, *"God loves you, Eddie. Come home, everything will be all right."*

"No, Eddie," the cornfield rebutted, its voice growing in strength. *"This is where you belong. The cornfield is your home."*

I looked up at the storm again. Black, deep green, and silver swirled together in a cloud that breathed and heaved in the sky. The storm seemed strangely alive. Beckoning.

In a voice that sounded like my own, the cornfield mocked, *"I'll earn it. I promise."*

But each time the brash voice spoke, it was countered by the comforting whisper. *"Come home."*

"I can't go home," I cried. "I don't even know how to get there from here."

The whisper said, "*Face the storm.*"

The cornfield responded immediately, as if panicked that I might listen to the whisper. "*The storm will crush you, Eddie. It destroys all who face it.*" The voice was gaining confidence by the minute, growing louder and stronger. "*Look around, Eddie, you are home. This is where you belong.*"

I looked around and knew the voice was right. This was the place I deserved to be. It offered no comfort, but at least I knew there wouldn't be any more pain.

239

"*You're worthy of so much more, Eddie.*" The gentle whisper was now barely audible. It knew it was losing. "*You just have to take the first step.*"

I was trapped. In front of me was a path to a storm that promised nothing but death. Behind me was a wall of shadow and regret. So there I stood,

Afraid to go forward . . .

And unable to go back.

Fifteen

he storm shrieked and groaned as I stared into it. I collapsed to my knees and began to cry again. But this time I didn't just cry, I *cried out.* "Mom!"

I saw her face in my mind. All of the guilt and anger and blame that had been building since Mom's death—and long before then—rushed out of me in a torrent. It took me a full minute to mix those few words into the sobbing, choking, and shuddering words that filled the air around me.

Then I prayed. "God," I cried, "everything I do, I screw

up. Please help me find a way to let everyone know how sorry I am for everything I've done and everything I've failed to do." Images of my mom and dad, grandmother and grandpa flashed quickly in my head. I didn't care about myself anymore; I was resigned to a life that looked a lot like the cornfield I was standing in, but I couldn't stand the thought of not being able to make amends for all that had happened.

I don't really know what I expected, but as I opened my eyes the world still looked exactly the same: predawn darkness, a wall of dead corn behind me, and the surreal, churning storm in front of me. A sickening, hopeless feeling filled my chest: *Maybe it's too late.*

As if in reply to my thoughts, the whisper spoke again. *"Face the storm, Eddie."*

Something rustled in the corn behind me. I spun around.

"Hello, Eddie."

It was a new voice, but it was strangely familiar. A man emerged from the blackness. The light from the storm's flashes offered me a quick glimpse of his face.

242

"Russell?" I wondered how long he'd been there.

"Is everything all right, Eddie?"

I rose from my knees and brushed myself off. "No."

"Where are you going?" he asked.

"Home."

Russell looked confused. "Then what are you doing here?"

"I'm lost."

"That's not exactly true."

I looked at him quizzically. "It's not?"

"No." Russell glared into my eyes. It was like he was looking through me. "You're exactly where you're supposed to be."

"What is this place?"

"It's the world you made for yourself."

"I made?" I didn't like being the author of such desolation and despair.

His piercing eyes fell on me. "Do you know how you got here?"

I was ashamed to tell him the truth. "I got into an accident on my bike, so I ran into this cornfield. Then the road vanished and the storm came."

"No, Eddie." Russell smiled gently and shook his head. "I mean, do you know how *you* got *here*?" This time the same words had an entirely different meaning.

The whisper prompted, "*When you choose the path, you choose the destination.*"

It hit me all at once. I knew. Little by little, mistake by mistake, I had put myself on a road whose destination had been inevitable.

Again came the whisper. "*All journeys, for good or evil, begin with one small step.*"

244   It had started that long-ago Christmas morning when I'd first seen the sweater. Right now that seemed like a thousand years ago. I nodded. "Yes, I know how I got here."

Russell's eyes panned the cornfield. "Most people find this place at some point. The darkness frightens them, but that's only because they have trouble seeing past it. If they could see what's just over the horizon, they'd realize how close to home they really are." His gaze settled back on me. "Do you know the way home?"

Russell asked questions for my sake, not his. I pointed toward the storm. "I think it's that way." My arm shook.

"How do you know that?"

"I don't know. I just do."

"Eddie, you made this world. But it's not yours. Go on home."

I looked at the storm and began to tremble. The winds howled, almost as if the storm sensed how vulnerable I was and how close I was to succumbing to it. Russell looked at me calmly. "You're right, it *looks* menacing." There was something comforting about his words. "It's amazing how bad things can look through the wrong eyes."

245

"The wrong eyes?"

"Yes, the wrong eyes. You're looking at the storm with the same eyes that you created it with."

I thought back to the mirror in my bedroom. Each time I'd looked into it over the last few months I'd had to look away as my own eyes had tried to reveal the truth: I hated myself *because* I blamed my problems on everyone and everything else.

Russell turned to face me. "Don't fear the storm, Eddie. Fear the cornfield. The cornfield may feel safe, but there is only cold and darkness here."

As if in defiance of his words, the storm began to howl even louder. The cornstalks bent under the power of its relentless winds, but, oddly, they leaned toward the storm, not away from it. *It's trying to pull them in, too.* I thought. Though the storm itself never moved, the noise emanating from its belly sounded like an approaching freight train. I covered my face.

Russell put his strong, weathered hand on my shoulder. His skin was warm. "It's okay, Eddie, the winds can't hurt you. Nothing can. Now face the storm."

A vicious gust of wind howled through the endless rows of dead cornstalks. "I can't, Russell. It's too big."

"You're bigger."

How could he say that?

Loose cornstalks were being uprooted by the storm's ferocious gusts. They mixed with dirt and debris and swirled all around us. Even though the noise was deafening, Russell didn't have to raise his voice, nor did I have to

246

strain to hear him. "You may not yet know who you are, Eddie, but I do. And I know that you are meant to walk through this storm. You weren't created to stand here in this cornfield. There's so much more waiting for you, and you're worthy of every ounce of it."

I swallowed hard, not believing him. "I can't, Russell, I'll just wait until it passes. I'm safe here."

His eyes blazed to life. He shook his head. "Oh, Eddie, you misunderstand. This storm will *never* pass. It can't. It's yours. Besides, life is not meant to be safe. It's only in our mistakes, our errors, and our faults that we grow and truly live. But you were right about one thing earlier: That is the way home. It's the *only* way home. But you *will* make it. Trust in me. Trust in *who* you really are."

"Who I am?" I said disparagingly. I was ashamed of the truth. "I'm nobody. I've hurt everybody who ever loved me."

"Sometimes the hardest part of the journey is believing that you're worthy of the trip."

Am I worthy? I thought to myself.

I looked back up at Russell. His gaze was strong and

247

infinitely loving. "Yes. Unquestionably, irrevocably, yes. Now go home."

I wanted to. But I was so weak. And the storm was so powerful.

"Trust, Eddie. The traveler's worthy of the journey. And he's worthy of the destination. Just take one small step on your own."

The storm looked even more ominous. My gaze was lost inside its giant, violent belly. *Trust.* I was weary of following my own will again—it's what had gotten me here. But, for once, I wanted to do the right thing.

I closed my eyes and took a step. It put me right in the very center of the storm. The shriek of its winds filled my ears. I wanted to cry out in fear, but I felt Russell take my hand. "Just one more step," he said, his calm voice far more powerful than the gale. *Trust.*

I closed my eyes and used all my might to shuffle my feet forward.

Silence.

I opened my eyes. We were on the other side of the storm. The sun was shining through from behind us, its golden rays reflecting off the menacing black clouds. It was so quiet that the chirping of birds and the rustling of leaves were the only sounds I could hear. What was once so dark was now bright, so refreshing, so peaceful. So warm.

"Where am I?" I looked around in wonder at the seemingly Technicolor corn, grass, and sky above me. It was the strangest, most wonderful palette of colors I'd ever seen. It was like a photographic reverse of the cornfield. Even the colors themselves seemed alive. *Is this heaven?*

Even though I had only thought the words, Russell shook his head. "You're on the other side of the storm. This is what awaits you. Not after you die, but once you start to really live."

"It's amazing." I looked at my guide. He was no longer dirty and old, but bright and ageless. "Who *are* you really, Russell?"

He smiled. "The real question is, *who are you?*"

Somehow I understood. Without the storm I couldn't know myself.

"Does everyone have to go through the storm?"

"Yes, sooner or later. But no one has ever been lost to

the storm, just lost *in* it. What most people don't realize is that you don't have to fight the storm, Eddie, you just have to stop feeding it—stop giving it power over you."

I looked around again. I tried to remember the smells, the sounds, the peacefulness, the happiness. The warmth. "If this isn't heaven, then what is it?"

"This is part of your journey. *Heaven* is different; it's even better." He spoke the word differently than I had ever before heard it. I realized that up to that point in my life, *heaven* had been more a myth than an actual place, kind of like a celestial version of Disneyland. It was a carrot waved to entice people to be good. But at that moment I realized the reality of the place and how much more there was to it.

"How is heaven different?"

"Heaven is the atonement of all things."

"Atonement?" I had heard the word at Grandma's church but never fully understood it.

"A-tone-ment," he said, punctuating the word. "It's a chance to fix the unfixable and to start all over again. It begins when you forgive yourself for all you've done wrong, and forgive others for all they've done to you. Your mistakes aren't mistakes anymore, they're just things that make you stronger. Atonement is the great redeeming and equalizing force that leads to the fulfillment of all things: every hug you've ever longed for, every Ferris wheel, baseball game, and walk in the snow you've missed. Everyone you've loved and lost. Atonement, Eddie, is heaven on earth."

"Then my mother and father are there . . . in heaven?"

The warmth of his eyes answered my question.

"Did they have to pass through the storm?"

"More times than you could know. But they had a great helper."

"You?"

He smiled. "No, Eddie. You. Their unending love for you helped them through the storm."

For the first time in as long as I could remember, I felt no guilt at hearing about my parents or the sacrifices they made for me. Only gratitude. I looked at Russell. "Will there be other storms?"

"Yes." Our eyes locked. "Unquestionably, irrevocably, yes."

251

"What if next time I'm too afraid?"

"I'll be with you," he said lovingly. "Remember, Eddie, no one who has passed through the storm has ever regretted the journey. No one ever stands here and wishes to go back to the other side."

"Thank you."

"Thank yourself. You made some good choices."

How good it felt to hear that.

"Now, Eddie, do you know who you are?"

252

With his words came a feeling of warmth and a joy so exquisite as to defy description. I realized that I was crying. I nodded.

A broad smile crossed his face. "Almost, you do. Almost." As I stared at him, I noticed that he had suddenly changed. A light now seemed to emanate from his skin. "You are joy, Eddie. You are joy."

He had a whiteness that I had never seen before. Brilliant. Beautiful. Warm. The light became so bright that I had to close my eyes and turn away—but in it I knew exactly who I was.

Sixteen

he smell of pancakes was so wonderfully strong that it actually woke me up. I opened my eyes and squinted at the bright light that was streaming through the bedroom window and across my face.

I touched my cheek. It was wet. I had been crying. Yes, I remembered that. *But how did I get back to the bedroom at my grandparents'? Had they come looking for me?* I noticed that I was fully dressed, but not in what I'd been wearing the night before.

As I gained consciousness, the world around me

flooded my senses. The brisk, sharp air of the upstairs room braced my skin. The aroma of doughy pancake batter and sweet maple syrup filled the air. I could hear the sound of sizzling bacon. Something was different about it all. I felt different. I felt light again.

I sat up. Two bread bags were lying on the floor, and my Christmas sweater was clutched tightly in my arms. I pressed it against my face. My mother had touched this sweater. Minute by minute and link by link she had made it. Not only had I changed, but so had the sweater. It felt different to me now—like a sacred relic of the past. "What a gift," I said to no one in particular. "What a perfect gift."

"Eddie?"

My heart stopped. I looked up at the closed bedroom door.

"Who are you talking to? May I come in?"

The door opened. My mother stood in its frame, illuminated in a bright halo by the light of the stairwell. At first I just stared, disbelieving. "Mom?"

"Good morning, sleepyhead."

256

I jumped from my bed and ran to her, throwing my arms around her and almost knocking her over. "Mom!"

She laughed. "My, I didn't expect such a big welcome. Especially after last night."

"You're here!"

"Of course I am. Did you think I left you?"

My eyes filled with fresh tears. "But we drove home . . . the accident."

She looked at me quizzically.

"When I came up to get you, you were sound asleep. I thought that after such a bad day it would be best to just let you sleep it off. Apparently I was right."

257

It was all coming back to me. I had come upstairs and lain down with my sweater for just a moment. . . . It couldn't have been a dream. Could it?

My mother ran her hand through my hair. "I thought maybe we would just try again in the morning. After all, isn't Christmas really about second chances?"

I pushed my head into her chest and cried. "Oh, Mom. Thank you. I'm so sorry about how I treated you. You're the best mother in the world. And I love my sweater more than you could ever know."

She took a step back, smiling. "Now, that was some night's rest. So you like your sweater now?"

"More than anything."

"More than, say, a bicycle?"

"A million times more. More than any stupid, old bicycle. Can we please do Christmas again? I'll do it right this time. I promise."

She looked at me and smiled. "You really do mean it, don't you?"

Unable to speak, I just nodded. She again pulled me into her and kissed the top of my head. "I love you."

I spoke through tears. "I know you do. That's why I love my sweater so much. Because you made it."

After a few more minutes she said, "Why don't you change your clothes and come downstairs. Breakfast is almost ready."

I held tightly to her. "Please don't leave."

She laughed. "I'm just going downstairs. And who knows, there might be other surprises."

Somehow, I knew what she was talking about. "I don't want any other surprises."

"Don't be too sure," she said. She kissed my forehead. "Get dressed and come on down. Grandma and Grandpa are waiting."

I wiped my eyes. "Okay."

She shut the door behind her. I quickly threw on my clothes and, of course, my sweater. While I was dressing, something outside the window caught my eye. A heavy white snow had started to fall. *Dad's snowfall,* I thought.

I reached the bottom of the stairs, and Grandma and Grandpa were watching me expectantly.

259

"Merry Christmas!" I said.

They furtively glanced at each other, no doubt wondering what had gotten into me.

"Merry Christmas to you," Grandpa said.

Grandma came over and gave me a hug. "Good morning, sweetheart. Merry Christmas."

"Eddie," my mother said. "Did you see the sn—" She stopped before she finished her sentence. She was staring at my sweater. "You really do like it."

"Best present I've ever got."

She looked the happiest I'd seen her in years.

"All right," Grandma said, carrying over a platter piled high with pancakes. "Let's eat."

As we took our seats around the table, I asked Grandpa if I could pray.

"By all means," he said.

We took each other's hands and bowed our heads.

"God, thank you for everything you've given us. For the time we have together. And for the miracle of Christmas. Thank you for the Atonement, the chance to start all over again. Help us to always remember who we are and to trust that we are worthy to make it through our storms. Amen."

As I looked up from the prayer, all the grown-ups were staring at me in wonder.

A few seconds passed before my mother finally broke the silence. "Dad, please pass the pancakes."

"Yes, dear."

He passed her the platter, but, as usual, Mom served me first. "Here, Eddie."

"Thanks," I said. "I'm starving. That was one *long* night."

Grandma gave me a puzzled look. "Long?"

"Eddie," Grandpa said, "while you were up in your room sawing logs, a man came by the house looking for you. Don't remember his name, but he said he saw a boy about your age out riding a bicycle. He wanted to make sure you were okay. I told him it couldn't have been you."

"Because I was asleep?" I asked.

"Well, that, and because you *don't* have a bicycle." A wry grin crossed his face. "Then again, who knows? We haven't looked everywhere yet. Should we go on a hunt?"

I smiled at him. "We can wait, Grandpa. Everything I really need is right here."

A broad smile filled my grandfather's face, and his eyes shone. "Well said, Eddie. Well said."

Shortly after breakfast, Grandpa led us all out to the barn. He was more excited than I was. With great fanfare, he unveiled the bike. Just as he himself had trained me, I acted surprised. I thanked everyone profusely, complimented Grandpa on his fine taste in two-wheelers, and asked how he'd been able to completely surprise me. In spite of my fine acting, Grandpa could tell that I'd known about the bicycle. I knew it irked him, since he didn't know how I could have found out. It was better than beating him at cards—which, of course, I couldn't have done, considering that all of the hearts from his favorite deck were wedged into the spokes.

Later that afternoon, as the snow fell peacefully outside, I lay near the fire next to my mom, listening to a Burl Ives Christmas record. She ran her long fingers through my hair. "This has been the most wonderful Christmas," she said wistfully.

"It has," I said. "Just like old times."

She laughed. "You're only twelve, Eddie. You don't have any 'old times.'"

We both laughed. Then I said, "Mom . . ."

"Yes?"

"Thank you for all you do for me. For how much you work and change your schedule to be with me."

"How did you know I did that?"

"I just don't say thank you enough."

She looked at me and her eyes filled. "Do you know why I do it, Eddie?"

"Why?"

"Because you're my greatest joy, Eddie. You're my joy."

263

The Way It Begins . . .

My grandfather's full name was Edward Lee Janssen, and he was indeed my summertime best friend. While the middle name on my birth certificate reads just "Lee," I've always insisted on using "Edward Lee" throughout my life. In fact, all of my friends, and even my children, believe that "Glenn Edward Lee Beck" is my legal name.

I am "Eddie," and I grew up in a small town called Mount Vernon, Washington. My mother's name was Mary, and she died when I was thirteen, not long after giving me a Christmas sweater that I threw on the floor.

My grandparents were very much like those described in the book. My grandfather was a great man and a great friend.

My father, though, was not missing in my life, as he was in this book. While he was always there for me, he and I were never close until later in life, when I sobered up, stopped feeling sorry for myself, and started to count my blessings. It was then that I called my father and told him that I didn't know how to be his son. He told me that he felt the same way, but added that if I would promise to sit through the awkward silence, we would figure it out. His words still bring tears to my eyes as I write them today.

I did as he asked, and I am so proud that we survived the awkward silences. My father has been the best friend I've ever had, and it has been the best fifteen years of our lives.

Our family bakery really was called City Bakery, and my father really was more like a craftsman than a baker. On a trip back home during the summer of 2007, I noticed that Mount Vernon's downtown was coming back to life. The mall that had driven shops like ours out of business had been torn down and replaced with an even bigger mall. I didn't go in; I'd already seen malls exactly like it in a hundred other towns.

Russell is a compilation of several of my life's most vital elements. There is a real man named Russell (minus the sepia tone), who lived next door to my grandparents. He has all the kindness and wisdom of a farmer who's worked with his hands his whole life. I decided to use him as a model for the character when, during that trip back home, I visited the street where my grandparents lived in Puyallup, Washington. Russell was still living next door, long after my grandparents had passed. He showed me a willow tree that he had planted from a branch my grandmother had given him when I was very small. It now shades his backyard.

Russell is also a grateful tip-of-the-hat to my dear friend Pat Gray. Many of you have heard me talk of him often on radio, TV, and in my stage shows. I met Pat later in life, and he guided me through some of my darkest days and gave me the greatest gift anyone can give: faith.

But the biggest part of Russell came from a dream

that I had in my midthirties. The cornfield scene was real for me, as was the color and warmth on the other side. It was sacred, and it completely changed my life. I believe this is the reason, as I told you in the prologue, that the book wrote itself.

While I didn't know at the time who Russell was in my dream, I feel that I do know now. But who he is *to you* is something that only you can decide.

That dream and Russell are not just mine, and neither is the cornfield. We all find ourselves there at some point. Yet I fear that far too many of us waste our lives standing in that darkness and cold because we can't put our past behind us and take that first step into the unknown. We either don't know, or don't believe, that there is beauty and happiness for us just on the other side of fear.

I am an alcoholic. I buried my guilt, pain, and feelings for so long that they would have killed me if I had not had this dream. I only wish it had happened when I was thirteen, like it did for Eddie.

Unfortunately, I had many more mistakes to make before I was driven to my knees and finally pled, "Your will,

268

not mine." I was in my midthirties and had been working on healing myself for more than a year. I thought I was making good progress, but it turns out there were places that I just wasn't willing to go.

I was tired. Tired of soul-searching, tired of remembering, tired of looking at things I'd spent a lifetime avoiding. Without consciously deciding to, I found myself willing to stand in the cornfield with just a few answers because it was off the highway and relatively safe. Yet, in retrospect, it was more.

269

I wonder sometimes how many of us don't face ourselves because we are convinced that we're worthy of only a certain level of happiness. We are limited by our imaginations and thoughts of worthiness and joy. We become comfortable in our misery because it is all we know. Or maybe it's just that we don't look for the "real" us because we're afraid that there isn't any real us to find.

One night I had a dream: The broken road. The dying cornfield. A storm unlike anyone should ever have to witness with their own eyes. Nowhere to go.

Then an old, mysterious man showed me the way.

I woke from this dream at three o'clock in the morning and immediately went to get my paints to try to re-create the scene on both sides of the storm. Despite my very best efforts, I just couldn't get it quite right. I have tried and failed many times since. I wonder if even in this book I have really captured the coldness of the cornfield, the true warmth of Eddie's experience on the other side of the storm, and the light of the stranger this book calls Russell.

Maybe it was never meant to be fully re-created. Just like in my dream, maybe we are supposed to see only a hint of the message and messenger and leave the rest to faith.

270

In the final pages Eddie is given a second chance. That, my friend, is a gift to *me* and from *me* to *you*. It is the real gift that I now see as represented by that last present I received from my mother. It is the understanding that you can be forgiven, that you can start over, and that if you face your greatest fears and regrets, the sky will open up and you will find happiness and love. It is the key to breaking the chain of regret and misery.

My mom gave me the sweater, but the greatest gift was

given to all of us by a loving Father in Heaven. It is the only true gift ever given to all and yet opened or appreciated by so few. It is the gift of redemption and atonement, and it sits on the top shelf, largely untouched, in the closets of our soul.

At Christmas we celebrate the birth of the Christ child, but by doing so, sometimes we miss the real meaning of the season. It is what that infant, boy, and then perfect man did at the end of His ministry that makes the birth so special.

Without His death, the birth is meaningless.

271

For years, I didn't believe in redemption as anything other than a word you hear from a preacher. I didn't think it was real. Even if it was, I didn't think I was worthy. That is a lie.

It is real.

It's not just a word; it is a life-changing force. I am worthy.

You are worthy.

We all are.

I guess the real lesson I learned that last Christmas

with my mother was that the greatest gift is any gift that is given with love. I so clearly remember the look in her eyes as she saw my sweater rolled up in a ball on the floor of my room, and I remember realizing all that she had done for that gift. I refuse to stand at His feet and see Him with the same look in His eyes as he asks me, "Son, is that the gift I gave you?"

Pick up your redemption. Cherish it. Wear it. Share it. It has the power to transform lives. *It has transformed mine.*

272

I finally know *who* I am, and I am happy. As I write these final words in bed well after 2:00 a.m. just outside New York City, I realize how many times I would have given anything to be able to live back on that simple street. My grandparents and everyone else who lived there still stand out as the most successful people I've ever met. They had everything they needed, but, more important, they wanted everything they had.

For much of my life I fought with guilt over the way I treated my childhood sweater and the events surrounding that Christmas morning. I could never give a sweater away, no matter how ugly, old, or small it was. I clung to drawers full of them, in every shape and size you can imagine.

Fortunately I got past that after I faced my storm. The old man in my dream was right once again: It wasn't as bad as I thought.

I eventually gave all my sweaters to Goodwill, and I am completely at peace with it. I found that I didn't need them anymore, because it's so warm here. . . .

It is just so warm.

Merry Christmas,
Glenn-Edward Lee-Beck

Acknowledgments

 find that every time I try to write ac-
knowledgments for a book, I end up feel-
ing just like my mother must've felt that Christmas
morning when I left my sweater in a ball on the floor. I
always hope not to disappoint, but I know that I always
will. As soon as I send this off to my publisher, more faces
and names that I'd somehow forgotten inevitably will
come to mind.

In some ways I guess it's a good problem to have. It's a
healthy reminder that I am on the other side of my storm
only because of all the amazing friends who've helped me

along the way. It's also a reminder that I play a very small role in my own success.

Thank you all for giving me the second greatest gifts there are: your trust, friendship, support, and, most important, your love.

Tania Beck

My children

All my parents

Claire McCabe

Pat Gray

Robert and Colleen
   Shelton

Roy Klingler and Family

Michelle Gray

Coletta Maier and Family

Jeff Chilson

David and Joanne Bauer

Jeremy and Makell Boyd

Bobby Dreese

Bruce Kelly

Jim Lago

Carma Sutherland

Robert and Juaniece
   Howell

Jon Huntsman

Bill Thomas

David Neeleman

Jaxson Hunter

Gary and Cathy Critten-
   den

My home ward

All my friends in Sumner,
   WA

Chris Balfe

Kevin Balfe

Stu Burguiere

Adam Clarke

Dan Andros

Rich Bonn

Liz Julis

Carolyn Polke

Joe Kerry

John Carney

Sarah Sullivan

Jeremy Price

Christina Guastella

Kelly Thompson

Kristyn Ort

Chris Brady

Nick Daley

Pat Balfe

Eric Chase

Conway Cliff

Virginia Leahy

John Bobey

My television and radio
  crews

My floor and makeup
  crew

Mark Mays

John Hogan

Charlie Rahilly

Dan Yukelson

Dan Metter

Julie Talbott

Gabe Hobbs

Kraig Kitchin

Brian Glicklich

George Hiltzik

Matthew Hiltzik

Dom Theodore

Carolyn Reidy

Louise Burke

Mitchell Ivers

Sheri Dew

Duane Ward

Joel Cheatwood

Jim Walton

Ken Jautz

Josanne Lopez

Lori Mooney

Greg Noack

The listeners, viewers, and
 readers

The insiders

City Bakery (1898–2006)

Richard Paul Evans

Jason Wright

Marcus Luttrell

Greg and Donna Stube

Paul and Angel Harvey

Thomas S. Monson

Russell Ballard

Neil Cavuto

Anderson Cooper

Brad Thor

Don Brenner

Albert Ahronheim

David Marcucci

Blake Ragghianti

Anthony Newett

278

A Special Message from Glenn

n *The Christmas Sweater*, Eddie's trials begin when his father succumbs to cancer. I didn't select that disease by accident. Almost all of us know someone who has been affected by it in some way, and I am no different; my grandfather had cancer. But I chose cancer for another reason as well—because of someone who I believe will cure it.

His name is Jon Huntsman, and I consider him a role model, an inspiration, and a friend.

Mr. Huntsman grew up in a two-room house with cardboard walls and outdoor plumbing. His family struggled for every penny they made and every bite of food they ate. But now, decades later, he's traded in that two-room shack for a spot on the Forbes 400 list. Mr. Huntsman is a billionaire.

While he may not be a household name, the products he's dreamed up over the years have changed the way we live. From the first Big Mac containers to egg cartons, to plastic bowls, dishes, and forks, Huntsman Chemical went from nothing to the largest privately held chemical company in the world.

282

But Jon Huntsman isn't an inspiration to me because of the amazing things his company has produced or how much money he's made. He's an inspiration for how much he's giving away: all of it.

Though involved in many charities, Mr. Huntsman's passion is the Huntsman Cancer Institute and Hospital that he founded in Salt Lake City. It's a place where patients are treated like family, and family members of patients are treated like royalty. But more important, it's a place where everyone is treated with love and respect—two things that are in short supply these days.

When I visited the institute for the first time, I told Mr. Huntsman that I'd never seen anything like it before. "I know," he replied, obviously used to hearing that kind of reaction. "We're going to cure cancer and then we're going to turn this place into a Ritz Carlton."

He smiled, and I wasn't sure if he was kidding or not. Then he looked at me with zeal in his eyes and determination on his face. "Glenn," he said firmly and without an ounce of hesitation, "we *are* going to cure cancer here." It wasn't what he said but how he said it—humble, almost casual, yet full of fierce and overwhelming confidence.

283

I believe him.

If your own success in life has made you fortunate enough to be able to help others, then please consider taking a look at the Huntsman Cancer Institute. Read about their mission and their facility, but, above all, read about Jon Huntsman, a self-made billionaire who intends to die penniless in the service of others. He is someone who has accomplished almost everything he has ever set his mind to, and I know he will accomplish that as well.

Mr. Huntsman has given away more than $1.2 billion

in the last decade. Yet no matter how broke he is when he eventually passes on, he will always be a living example of Russell. And he will always be the richest man I've ever met.

—Glenn

For more information, please visit
www.huntsmanscancerfoundation.org.